GOING ROGUE

A Tactical Operations & Protection (TOP) Prequel

Blye Donovan

BOOKS BY BLYE DONOVAN

Rolling Brook Series
Hunted at Whiteford Farm
Gifts from a Stalker
Small Town Frame-up
Condemned by Secrets
Marked as Queen of Hearts

Stand-alone Novels
Undercover Santa
Blaze of Glory

Texas Heat Shared Series
Wait for You

TOP Security Series
Going Rogue

ISBN: 979-8-9867683-7-3
Imprint: Independently published.
Cover designed by Blye Donovan. Title graphic by BOOKCOVER4U.

For all the brave souls who have answered the call of duty.

CONTENT WARNING

This book contains profanity, violence, and mature sexual content. It also mentions attempted sexual assault.

CHAPTER 1

Rogue

The metallic taste of blood coated Rogan "Rogue" Shaw's tongue, mixing with salt from her sweat as she leaned her head back against the abrasive cell wall. Jagged points made by uneven crevices worn into the sand-colored brick pulled at her light blonde hair, but she didn't feel the sting. Blood dripped down her chin from the split in her lower lip. She swiped at it, and a white-hot determination flooded her system, reddening her tanned face in the dry summer heat.

None of it showed in her expression, though. There, she appeared defeated—ready to submit to whatever demands they made on her. But it was an act. One she hoped would make her captors let down their guard. At least enough for her to escape.

Because she *would* be getting out of here. The only question was *when.*

Shifting to find a more comfortable seat on the packed dirt floor, Rogue pulled her cargo-clad legs into her chest. She had a solid plan. She just needed events to fall into place; then, she'd be free. Preferably before another one of those ignorant fucks tried to have their way with her—again.

Rogue barely contained the growl rising up her throat. No matter that she'd have been happy to leave her V-card behind a long time ago, this wasn't how she intended to lose it.

Nor did she intend to die in this prison cell.

The little family she had left might not understand why she'd put herself in a position to be captured in the first place, but if she didn't make it home, they'd mourn her loss. Or, at least, she hoped they would.

She didn't fight to stay alive for them. She did it for herself. For the life she'd barely had the chance to live yet.

Thinking about the attack, she gently touched a knuckle to her lip and had to hide a wince. It came away red with her blood. The sight added fuel to the promise she'd already made. The bastard who'd come at her would be the first to die. She'd already bruised his balls, but he had a whole other level of pain coming for him when her hands were unbound.

Lowering them between her pulled-up knees, she tugged her wrists apart, but they barely moved. The asshole who'd tied them knew how to knot a fucking rope.

With brown eyes blazing, she glared down at it. The knot wasn't a complex Navy one. Those she knew from her time in the service and could've easily undone. Bending her head, she tugged at the rope with her teeth, which only made the fibers cut into her skin. The abrasive material rubbed across the slash in her lip, making her hiss. Anger at her situation had her pulling against the binding until it carved blood-red marks around her wrists.

She'd left the military because she'd been tired of sitting on the sidelines while operators carried out the missions *she'd* planned.

Look where it got you.

The knot didn't lessen; it held tight as fuck. Undoing it would take time. Time Rogan wasn't sure she had.

A scuffle sounded in the hall as if to prove her point, and her whole body tensed for a fight. It had only been a half hour since the last man left. She'd hoped for a longer break before she had to defend herself again.

Adrenaline coursed through her veins, pumping so fast her heart galloped like a prized filly about to cross the finish line. Despite her best efforts to appear docile and calm, she had to be visibly vibrating.

Dropping her head to her knees, she hoped it looked like she sobbed quietly, not like she chomped at the bit to bite one of those mother-fucking militants' heads off. Because she did.

"Rogue?" Her gaze whipped up at the whispered word.

Whiskey-Tango-Foxtrot?

"Crane?" She knew the man who stood outside her cell from his voice alone. The richness of his tone never failed to strike a chord within her body, stirring something she'd rather not examine too closely.

Jumping to her feet, Rogue stared into the familiar caramel eyes attached to the baritone. It didn't matter that a tan balaclava covered his face. Underneath it, his close-cropped hair would be black as night, and his cheekbones sharp. The fabric outlined the square cut of his jaw but hid the cleft in his chin, where a small scar ran diagonally across it.

She took in his tan boots, desert camo cargo pants, and khaki t-shirt covered by his black tactical vest. He'd worn the same outfit the last time she saw him. "What are you doing here?"

Instead of answering, his golden-brown eyes swept her face and went tight. "Step back," he growled in a low manner which made her react without thinking.

From the far wall of her cell, Rogue watched him pack the lock on her door with C-4. Knowing it would make a hell of a noise and draw too much attention, she opened her mouth and hissed, "They'll hear that all the way to Syria, dumbass."

He merely grinned. "Nice to see your time here hasn't sweetened you up."

Before she could retort, a distant explosion rumbled through the cell walls.

"And that's our cue, squirrel."

She rolled her eyes at the nickname. It was short for 'secret squirrel' due to her background in intelligence. She hated it, and he knew it.

Crane lost the teasing expression, and she covered her ears. With a nod, he blew open the door to her cage. At the same time, a closer explosion shook their building. Whatever he'd done, there was a good chance the noise from it covered the detonation on her door. She could give him props for the distraction—later.

Through the haze of smoke and debris, Crane appeared. As he cut her hands free, the smell of diesel and a hint of burnt plastic filled her nose but layered within it; his distinct masculine scent penetrated—infuriating and comforting all at once.

Staring into the honey of his eyes, something in her wavered, desperate to lean into his woodsy smell and the broad chest it came from, but she walled off those thoughts before they became more dangerous.

Rogue shook her head as a shockwave from another explosion hit the cell. Then, distant yelling reached her ears.

Crane heard it, too, because he morphed into rescuer mode. "Time to go."

Before she could stop him, he'd lifted and slung her over his shoulder like she weighed less than a feather.

"Hey!" She beat her fists against his back, and it felt like pounding on a rock. "I can walk, you know!" At a muscular five feet, eight inches, she topped out at 160 pounds, but she almost felt light, anchored on his six-five frame.

"No need, squirrel." He slapped her ass with a playful smack. "We're going to fly."

* * *

Crane

"This is what you call flying?"

Rogue's question mocked him as he replaced the magazine in his Glock, but

Miles "Crane" Burkhart didn't mind the ribbing. He was just happy she remained alive to give it to him. When she'd been captured . . . he feared the worst.

"Not exactly." He gave her a wink despite the snag in his rescue mission. The plane he'd been going to charter was late. A glance at his disposable phone showed what he already knew—radio silence. "But I have a Plan B."

Always leave yourself an out. It was their team's motto, and when Rogue had gotten captured, they'd taken it.

The fact they had twisted in Crane's gut like sour meat as he secured his spent clip to his tactical vest. He and Rogue worked for Tactical Operations & Protection, or TOP, as it was known in the business. They were modern-day soldiers for hire, so he supposed he shouldn't be surprised the rest of the team had viewed her capture as an acceptable loss for the sake of the operation.

But Crane hadn't been able to let Rogue go so easily. He'd tried the 'every man for himself' thing, but his years as a Marine were too ingrained. You don't leave your brothers—or sisters, in this case—behind.

Sister. Right. He had a lot of thoughts about Rogue but none of them were brotherly. As the middle child with an older brother and baby sister, he knew a thing or two about siblings. And that's *not* how he viewed Rogue.

Crane glanced over at her, where she knelt behind a stack of packing crates.

Filled with assault rifles, no doubt.

He didn't know this rag-tag group of militants, but it was clear to him they wanted to join the terrorists desolating the rest of Iraq. He figured the cargo he and Rogue hid behind, plus the other crates he'd blown sky high, had been a buy-in. Since the fuckers had kept her alive, he gathered she'd been meant as part of the bargain.

Even in her roughed-up state, she was gorgeous. Though he sweltered under the balaclava, she glowed with the early evening sun beating down on her. Her pale golden strands reminded him of the angel Christmas tree topper he'd grown up with.

The thought made him smile, which she caught when she glared at him. "What the hell is Plan B?"

Her hair might be angelic, but those eyes were all sin—like a deep, dark rum he wanted to taste. He'd been dying to kiss her since she'd walked into TOP headquarters two years ago. Of course, she'd shot down any advance he'd made. But he got it.

She didn't want to shit where she ate.

Even if sex with her would be off the charts, she was right. Sex led to entanglements, and in their business, those could get you killed.

An uncommon frown pulled at the corners of Crane's mouth. His coming back for her *was* an entanglement . . . and they hadn't even experienced the good parts yet. *Fuck.*

He didn't know what this meant for either of their positions on the team or if they'd even be allowed back in after he disobeyed orders to get the hell out of Dodge.

"Earth to Crane." Rogue poked the center of his forehead, and he blinked to see she'd moved much closer.

Damn. Underneath the dirt and sweat, he could still smell her signature scent. It always made him think of cinnamon or spicy vanilla. The fragrance lingered in his thoughts and never failed to make him ache.

"If you're not going to use that, I'll take it."

When she reached for his gun, he grabbed her arm. "Nice try, squir—" At her wince, he loosened his grip. It might be 100-plus degrees, but that heat had nothing to do with the blood boiling in his veins as he stared down at the raw skin of her wrists.

Something dark stirred in his gut. A scorpion roused from its slumber under the sand.

"Sorry." His thumb barely brushed the rope burns, and he had the strangest urge to kiss each hurt.

At the same time, Crane wanted to pop each and every one of these fuckers for the burns alone. Cold-blooded instinct pulled his eyes to the split on her lip, and his jaw tightened. They were *all* dead men walking.

"It's fine." She tugged her arm away, and he released her. "Plan B?"

At her arched brow, he let it go. Not because she'd brushed it off but because he couldn't think about what else Rogue might have gone through if he wanted to keep a clear enough head to get them both out of here alive. "Hide."

"Hide? That's your Plan B?" She growled the question at him, baring her teeth, and he admired the way her eyes fired with incredulity. "This isn't a fucking game! I'm not waiting around for them to seek us out."

Granted, she was right. He didn't like the idea of waiting to be found either, but it would be dark in a couple of hours. They could use the darkness to their advantage. "Just 'til the sun goes down. Then we egress."

He watched her work through their situation in her head. Her nose scrunched, highlighting the dusting of freckles across its bridge. The expression looked cute on her, and Crane fought back another smile. He couldn't seem to stop now that he'd freed her. They might be far from safe, but he had every confidence they'd make it out of this shithole country in one piece.

She blinked, her rum-colored eyes glinting. "Fine. I know the perfect place."

CHAPTER 2

Rogue

It stank to high heaven in here. Rogue hoped the ferocity of the smell would keep the militants away while she and Crane hid.

"Holy fuck. I'm going to lose my lunch." Gagging noises emitted from his throat as he shuffled into the cargo trailer behind her.

She couldn't tell if the heaving was real or feigned, but she understood the sentiment. "Go ahead. It'll improve the smell." The statement oozed sarcasm, and she rolled her eyes.

They'd crept around several piles of bagged fertilizer to enter the container. The smelly stuff had probably been transported inside it, but the militants had been smart enough not to leave something so potentially toxic baking inside a metal box. Even with the ventilation fan installed, this thing would heat up fast under the desert sun.

Over a hundred 40-pound bags had to be stacked around the trailer she and Crane had crept into. The militants weren't using it to plant an herb garden in the desert. Fertilizer contained ammonium nitrate. Add a little fuel, some flame, and it became highly combustible.

Heading toward the back of the trailer, she used the flashlight she'd borrowed from Crane to navigate. No moonlight filtered in through the ventilation fan, and the inside of the container became nearly pitch-black as soon as they'd closed the door.

A sweep with her light confirmed what she'd discovered earlier. The rectangular trailer that companies used to transport goods on eighteen-wheelers or cargo ships remained empty. These boxes littered the militants' compound, but this one had been placed as far from the main buildings as possible.

Likely because of the stench.

Fertilizer smelled fragrant regardless, but cooking it under the desert's scorching heat . . . Yeah, a stuffy nose would've been welcome right about now. She checked the vent and ensured the fan was running. While poisoning the militants sounded like a good idea, she didn't want to subject herself and Crane to that fate.

"My eyes are fuckin' watering." Crane slung the assault rifle he'd nabbed from a militant he neutralized onto his back and pressed his fingers into his sockets.

"Are you still whining?" Rogue shook her head and pulled him further away from the nasty stuff sitting outside. "You're the one who wanted to hide." He'd blown her original escape plan to smithereens, so she didn't see another route out of there.

Despite the change in her plan, a part of her preferred this—not being alone—though she wouldn't admit it to *him*.

Since they were going to be in the container for a while, she placed the flashlight on the ground, standing up, with its beam shining between them.

Crane dropped his hands and shot her a

look that screamed disbelief. "And this is the best option?"

Cozying up next to so much explosive material might be a risky choice, but they only needed a couple of hours. "Yes." She couldn't help the evil grin teasing at her lips. Crossing her arms, she arched a brow. "You think any of them want to come out here, either?"

The tight lines around his mouth twitched until a chuckle broke free. "How'd you know this was here?"

"Found it when we were searching for the target." She shrugged and tried not to think about the shitshow of an op that landed them in this situation. Experience had taught her to trust her gut, and it had been rebelling before they started this mission. Something had been off . . . she just hadn't known what.

Shaking away the feeling she'd ignored, Rogue met Crane's gaze and explained, "I thought this might be a holding cell because of its remote location." Her voice strangled with emotion before she added, "I was wrong."

When his eyes softened and he stepped toward her, she backed into the wall. She didn't want pity; she wanted justice. Her stomach churned with fiery rage over what she'd been through in the last twelve hours. It burned up her throat as she growled in a low voice, "What the hell happened?"

Their team had infiltrated the militant's base to find and extract an American who aided terrorists. The intel they'd been fed claimed this group had captured him despite his supposedly being on their side. The job Tactical Operations & Protection had been tasked with required them to turn the traitor over to the authorities in the U.S. so he could stand trial for his crimes. It should have been a quick grab-and-go, but that wasn't the way it went down.

"He wasn't here."

"Tell me something I don't know, Crane. I saw their cell block, remember?" She wanted to scream her frustration but could only whisper-shout at him. No need to give away their location to the men who wanted them dead.

"Hey, squirrel. Don't bite *my* head off. I

came back to help you." His low rumble and earnest stare didn't sway her.

Rogue straightened and stared him down. "Why?"

TOP was all about the money. The one thing she trusted was her team members would do whatever proved necessary to ensure the mission's success so they could cash in. The minute the op had gone sour, they lost that opportunity. She hadn't expected them to come back for her. But here stood Crane.

What is he getting out of saving me?

Instead of breaking her gaze and giving some non-answer to hide the truth, he surprised her. Little alarm bells went off as those caramel eyes darkened, and he stepped into her space, practically caging her against the wall. Her leg twitched, ready to knee him in the balls if necessary.

He'd pulled the balaclava off and his dark head gleamed with sweat as he tilted it toward her. "Do you really have to ask?" His eyes burned into hers, a curious mixture of anger and relief.

She swallowed around the sudden knot in

her throat as his musky scent surrounded her. Team member or not, he'd always had the ability to put her on edge. They'd been working together for two years. She couldn't say she'd gotten close to anyone on her team, but there'd always been . . . *something* between her and Crane. An energy that pulled them together every time she tried to push them apart.

Like magnets.

She felt his eyes on her whenever they'd been in the same room. Staring into them now, she said, "I knew the risks."

His hands lifted, but instead of reaching for her, he placed them against the wall on either side of her head.

To intimidate? She wasn't sure. Her muscles tensed in anticipation but not of a fight.

Squaring her shoulders, she told him the truth. "I didn't expect a rescue from any of you."

As the only female on the team, she fought constantly for acceptance. One member in particular had even made it clear he didn't like having her along for the ride.

Jordan had told her a woman on the team was a liability, and she hated that he'd think her current predicament proved him right.

He had to be former CIA. Not that he'd ever said. Most of the rest of the team was prior military like Crane. Either special forces or spec-ops, and a couple hard-liners still weren't sure she could hack it. But she *would* prove them wrong . . .

"Maybe you should've." Crane gritted the words out, and she stood close enough to see the muscle in his jaw work before he said, "Cinnamon and vanilla. Even with the smell of shit around us, I can't get you out of my lungs."

Over the course of their time working together, she'd seen him angry, but he wore an easygoing attitude more often than not. He'd hit on her in the beginning, but after she'd turned him down, he seemed to have gotten the message that she wasn't interested.

She didn't really date; plus they worked together, which made him off-limits.

She'd lived by the rule since her time in the military. Being a woman in charge of a group of men could be a precarious position. It meant she'd never wanted to do anything to compromise herself in their eyes. Respect was too important to sacrifice for lust. But truthfully, she'd never been tempted to cross the line . . . *until* Crane.

He never failed to tease her and call her the grating nickname—Squirrel. But this . . . this side of him felt different. It only made her more wary.

"And that's my fault, how?" she bit out, ignoring the stirring in her belly at having him hovering over her close enough to—

"Rogue . . ." He sucked in an audible breath.

Breathing in my scent or steadying himself? Her analytical brain couldn't help wondering.

"Would you have left *me* behind?"

Her stomach cramped on the question. She opened her mouth to tell him yes, but the word refused to come out. Instead, she shot him a glare hot enough it could've peeled paint.

A smirk tilted the corner of his lips as he pushed off the wall. "That's what I thought."

* * *

Crane

The attraction wasn't one-sided. One of these times, Crane would make Rogue do something about it. But he wouldn't push now with her lip swollen and after she'd been through . . . *fuck*. His whole body vibrated with barely controlled rage when he dared to think what she might've already had to endure.

Hands fisted and jaw clenched, he turned away to get himself under control. Because he had to ask her. Had to *know*.

"The rest of the team?" Though her voice hadn't cracked on the question, he caught the sense of betrayal layering it. He wasn't too happy with the rest of TOP right now, either.

Mouth thinning, he gave her a slight shake of the head. "I'm sorry I couldn't come sooner." The hours he'd waited putting his rescue mission into action were slowly burning through his gut. What had she been through while he'd planned? His teeth clenched so tightly he was surprised he didn't crack his jaw.

I should've come sooner.

The thought had been bombarding him all day, but he didn't stop to question why her capture made him so upset.

"Where are they?"

He blinked, pulling himself back to the present to focus on what she'd asked. She was alive and safe . . . for now.

The team had moved to a secure location to regroup. He knew what she thought—the two of them should head to wherever TOP had holed up. That had been his plan, but without any messages from the contact who was supposed to be their ticket out of here, Crane didn't know if the team would even be in the same place by the time he and Rogue made it to them.

On a sigh, he pinched the bridge of his nose, where a headache brewed, and answered, "A safehouse near Al Asad Airbase." He faced her and wished he could soften the blow of his next words. "I don't know how long they'll stay there and with our flight out of here questionable . . ."

Rogue had been an intelligence officer. He knew she had brains to spare, and he could tell by her expression she understood what he hadn't said.

We're likely on our own.

Her cold stare didn't falter, but he glimpsed the anger burning in the pits of her eyes. His gut twisted as he reached for her face. She didn't flinch when he brushed a thumb across her split lip. "What did they do to you, Rogan?"

She turned her face away, but not before he caught the shine of unshed tears. Fresh anger surged through him, and a growl nearly left his throat. He'd kill any of them who'd touched her.

When she spoke, her voice was a whisper. "I hurt them more than they hurt me."

The breath had backed up in his lungs, but he blew it out now, even trying for a smile. If he didn't calm the fuck down, he wouldn't be of much use. "That's my squirrel."

At the nickname, she met his gaze. Something he couldn't decipher hid in those dark depths. But as quick as he'd glimpsed it, it dissipated into exasperation as she said, "Don't call me that."

On a deep breath, he let go of the tension riding his muscles. A sly grin quirked the corners of his mouth as he tried to lighten the mood. "Why? It suits you." She could be as cute and wily as the furry little animal.

She let out a scoff. "Wow, how flattering."

A low chuckle shook Crane's chest. His code name came from a bird and had to do with his long legs. Not exactly flattering, either. He hadn't picked the name himself. If he'd had the opportunity, he'd have gone with something cool like Ghost or Cobra.

Unbothered by her reaction, Crane continued to tease her. "But squirrels are cute."

Her eyes sparked with indignation and her hands inched toward a weapon she didn't carry. When she remembered, she scowled. The fierce look only made her more attractive.

Just like that, the teasing shifted.

Damned if he didn't want to kiss the expression off her face. His blood sang, being so close to her, and he desperately needed a taste of her smart mouth.

He leaned in and trailed a knuckle down her cheek. "You want flattery, Rogue?" Bending his head, he stopped a breath away. "I've been thinking about this for two years. No matter what I do, there's only you." Carefully, he closed the distance and placed his mouth over hers in a gentle kiss, mindful of putting pressure on her injured lip.

Her lingering sweet and spice-tinged scent filled his nose. He had a moment to hope he didn't hurt her, another to want to dive inside and really taste her. But the kiss lasted for maybe two point five seconds before he felt her leg move and shifted aside so that her kick hit his thigh, not the jewels she'd been going for. Breathing harder than the slight caress warranted, he waited for her to respond.

"If we can't fly out of here, we need a new plan."

Crane cocked a brow at her change in subject. Was she not going to acknowledge their kiss and ignore what he'd just said?

For once, her face gave nothing away, leaving him with no clue what she felt or thought.

Appears so.

At her brushoff, a frown creased his forehead. He didn't get how she could be so unaffected when his whole body came alive whenever she drew near. Enough that, he began to wonder if what he felt for her was more than merely attraction.

Acknowledging the effect she had on him upped its potency, and an ache rocked his chest like a sliver of ice bored into it. The cold straightened his spine, and he backed up to lean against the adjacent wall. If she could be all business, so could he. "Yeah."

Without the plane his contact promised, they needed another mode of transportation because trekking across the desert on foot was suicide. If the environment didn't kill them, there were bound to be trigger-happy militants who would.

"Any ideas?" She crossed her arms and barked.

Right. Because it was *his* fault they were in this mess. At least, that's the message she broadcasted. But she'd asked the question with enough frost to make him wonder if she hadn't been so unaffected by the kiss after all.

Saving it to ponder later, he answered, "We could steal one of their dirt bikes or a truck."

Her mouth pursed in thought, but she asked, "And what's to keep them from coming after us?"

A risky plan popped in Crane's head. Then a feral grin twisted his lips in response as he pointedly glanced at the door to the container. "We put the fertilizer to good use."

CHAPTER 3

Rogue

What the fuck was that *about?*

Rogue tried her damnedest not to pick apart the kiss with Crane, but it wasn't in her makeup to let it go. Of course, she couldn't have *him* knowing that. Fuming over the whole debacle, she shot a glare in his direction. They traversed the compound, staying out of the meager glow cast by the lights gracing the camp. Barely more than a handful of rudimentary poles held electrical bulbs, which penetrated the dark, moonless night.

At least her frustration kept her warm in the cool night air. The summer sun had finally made its descent, dropping the temperature to a brisk 80 degrees. After acclimating to the hundred-plus temps during the day, eighty actually felt cold especially when she wore only a black tank top and cargo pants. When she'd been locked up, the militants had taken her jacket, vest, and the weapons stored in it.

Pushing the memory away, she suppressed a shiver as a breeze kicked dust into her face. As soon as they'd had the cover of darkness, they'd started positioning the explosives they'd fashioned from the fertilizer, some diesel they'd commandeered, and Crane's remaining C-4. Once they had everything in place, it'd be time to light them and get the hell off this compound.

Though she couldn't see Crane clearly, she felt him hulking a few feet in front of her. His presence wasn't unwelcome even if his kiss had been.

Hadn't it?

Rogue cursed herself for letting it distract her. While her hands were busy with her task, her mind kept examining their liplock. You'd think she'd never been kissed before the way she couldn't stop thinking about his mouth on hers. She had, of course, but none had ever lingered in her thoughts like this.

She'd be lying if she said it hadn't affected her. Her lips still tingled when she replayed it.

Because his gentleness had surprised her.

Crane was a Marine in the best possible way. Still, all that ego and testosterone meant she hadn't expected anything but a bruising crush of lips. The fact it hadn't been made her wonder what more he might be capable of. Which was a dangerous fucking turn of her thoughts.

At 27, she remained a virgin. She hadn't intentionally avoided relationships, but she'd never sought them out, either. Somehow, she'd always been working; before then, studying had been the excuse she used too often in college.

Her friends had fallen in love and then moped when their hearts were broken. She'd known they all thought of her as a frosty bitch. It had been unfair, but she let it stand. It was easier that way because she had to keep her heart safe from ever crossing the line into love.

An uncomfortable weight settled around her chest and pulled like an invisible rope, tightening with each breath.

She'd become a champion at pushing people away.

If you never let them get too close, they couldn't disappoint you . . . Her dad had taught her that. At age eleven, her parents divorced, but it hadn't been solely her mother that her father didn't want anymore; it had been his daughter, too.

Focus, Rogue.

She scolded herself as she crouched under a militant's truck, shaking off her line of thinking. It only ever led to bitterness, and she had more important things to stew over than her absent father. Like Crane's kiss.

Distracted, she smashed her finger between the ground and two bags of fertilizer. Something sharp cut into her hand, and she silently cursed. When she freed her hand from underneath the bags, blood dripped from a small puncture on her ring finger's tip. She must've managed to stab herself with a rock.

Hoping she didn't leave a trail, she clutched her palm into a fist and prayed it clotted soon. She didn't have time to stop and tend to it. Not with the whole compound on high alert after her breakout. The gate proved heavily guarded as if they knew their escapee would make a run for it at some point. That's why several bags of fertilizer wound up at the guard shack by the entrance.

With the assholes inside none the wiser.

A snicker tickled her throat. The big guy signaled with a sound, and she crawled out of her hiding spot, leaving behind a nice pile of explosive material. For being six-five, she had to give Crane props for moving as stealthy as a ghost. He managed to blend with the shadows, perhaps better than her, and she was damned stellar at it if she did say so herself.

She'd borrowed his balaclava to hide her bright hair but still felt overly exposed without her vest and gear. He'd given her his Glock, but she missed her own gun. Who knew what the militants had done with it? She didn't want to waste time looking. Her primary objective was to get out of this hellhole alive and hunting down equipment she could repurchase wasn't worth the risk.

Neither is a relationship with Crane.

The thought flashed in her head like a warning sign. It was bound to get messy when they worked together. So she'd avoided him since she'd joined the team with Tactical Operations & Protection.

A deep scowl twisted her lips as she tagged his shoulder to let him know she still followed. His quick squeeze of her fingers in response sent a tingle racing up her arm. Not at all happy about it, she jerked her hand away.

Why kiss me now?

He'd either been messing with her, and she knew the idiot could turn anything into a joke. *Or* he'd actually waited two years to kiss her. That option seemed unlikely.

Didn't it?

Because who does that? Who waits two years to make a fucking move? Wondering about it heightened her anger, adding to the adrenaline surging through her veins. Beneath the balaclava, the corners of her eyes crinkled with the desire to interrogate him.

I need answers.

Following behind Crane, she promised to do just that as soon as they were safe.

After what felt like an eternity, they placed the last explosive device. They'd spent the past hour marking several buildings and all the vehicles they could—except the one they planned to drive out of there—with fertilizer bombs. They'd had to be strategic in their choices to avoid detection and save as much time as possible.

She'd wanted to split up so they could cover more ground more quickly, but he'd refused to leave her side. She didn't know what had changed since yesterday, but Crane was acting differently toward her.

Protective in a way he hadn't before.

Like he didn't see her as part of the team anymore but a damsel in need of rescuing, which pissed her off. Her body hummed like the charges ready to go off. She was seconds away from calling him on it when a shout in Arabic pierced the still, evening air.

Before she could process what it meant,

Crane pulled her behind a cargo trailer and pushed her back against it. He moved in front of her until she felt the rough material of his tactical vest poking into her chest, effectively blocking her body with his.

"What the hell are you doing?" An outraged hiss left her throat with the question as she glared at the back of his head.

When he said nothing and checked his weapon, she tried another tactic. "We can't stop. We need to light the charges and egress like our lives depend on it because, oh yeah, they fucking do." She'd meant to sound calmer, but desperation to get off this compound made any chance of that impossible.

His answer came as a low grumble she had to strain to hear. "Trust me, squirrel."

What kind of answer is that?

Her body buzzed with adrenaline, but she made herself take a calming breath. "What did they shout?" She spoke Arabic, but Crane had a stronger grasp of the different dialects.

Again, she had to strain to hear his

response. "One of the militants found a fertilizer bag."

The adrenaline coursing through her body surged with a powerful jolt, and she lost any pretense of calm. "Then we need to move. Now!"

* * *

Crane

Rogue was right. They should be accelerating their plan, not pausing here to be found. But the fact she didn't have a bulletproof vest any longer damn near paralyzed him. Crane didn't want to take the chance of her getting shot.

His brain told his legs to move, but he wouldn't—couldn't—leave her vulnerable if the militants were onto them.

He felt her shift position and backed further into her. "Stay put." He knew she wasn't likely to listen, so he added a strained, "Please, Rogue," hoping she'd cooperate.

They were close enough that he felt her sigh of acceptance. It did little to ease the worry gripping his muscles, though. His ears perked for any movement in their direction.

At least the adrenaline pumping through his body heightened his senses. While he strained to listen for threats, her sweetly spicy fragrance overpowered any other scent.

Trying his best to ignore it, Crane gripped the Ka-Bar in his palm even tighter. If they were about to have company, he wanted to deal with it as quietly as possible, or they'd be well and truly fucked.

Seconds passed with nothing except the hammering of his pulse in his ears.

We should move.

Rogue had to be getting restless, but some instinct froze him in place.

One breath.

Two.

Then, a heated discussion between two men in Arabic reached them. It grew louder the closer the militants came to their position.

The men argued about the fertilizer and were likely on their way to check the area by the cargo container it had been transported in. Another heartbeat, and they drew closer. Crane felt Rogue's sharp intake of breath and shifted his feet into a better fighting stance.

They were going to be in a lot of shit when the militants found most of the fertilizer gone . . . unless he took out these fuckers before they realized.

Ready to do it, Crane eased his hold on Rogue, trusting she'd stay put.

Big fucking mistake.

As soon as he no longer restrained her, she took off, darting between containers like a cat. His bowels seized as if he was about to shit a brick. Cursing, he kept his eyes trained on her shadow, tracking her as the militants walked past his position, but he couldn't do anything about them now. He had no choice but to follow Rogue or lose her in the dark.

Anger rose to match the fear she'd triggered in him. The rapid rise and fall of his chest didn't ease when he reached her. Gripping her elbow, he growled in her ear. "What the hell are you doing? I was going to take out those tangoes."

She jerked her arm away with a grunt. "Putting our plan in motion. We don't have time to waste."

When he thought she'd take off again, she turned and gripped his forearm. "We're going to have to split up. I'll take what we planted on the western half of the compound. You take the east. We meet at the truck."

In reflex, a protest started up his throat, but he swallowed it because it had become their only option now that the militants were about to discover what they'd done. But damned if the thought of letting her go it alone didn't break him out in cold sweats.

Something suspiciously like panic crept up his back as he worked to unclench his jaw. *Dammit. Dammit. Dammit.*

Right now was not the time to lose his shit. Too much was at stake. "Rogue . . ."

God, he wanted to kiss her, hold her, never let her out of his sight.

Instead, he settled for a quick embrace. With his arms around her, it became even harder to let go.

But he had to.

Kissing the top of her head, he released her with a stern demand. "Don't die."

He caught a flash of her bright teeth. Then she said, "You either."

Before she could leave him there with his chest gaping open, he stopped her. "Wait." Taking off his tactical vest, he placed it in her hands. "Wear this." It would be a little big but better than sending her out there—alone—with no protection.

He could sense her consternation. "But what about you?"

When she made no move to put on the bulletproof vest, he helped her into it. "You wear it or we're not separating."

"But—"

As his fingers fastened the straps, he cut her off, "I'll be fine. And this way, I'm not distracted worrying about you."

At his admission, she didn't say anything else in protest. When he'd secured the vest as tight as it would go, she squeezed his hand before melting into the night.

Balling his palm into a fist as if he could sear her touch into his skin, he watched her disappear and prayed he wouldn't live to regret his decision to let her out of his sight.

CHAPTER 4

Rogue

Rogue had nearly reached the escape vehicle when explosions started popping off in a beautiful symphony of fire and destruction. She'd lit her last fertilizer bomb, but the blasts rising in a swelling crescendo across the compound came from Crane's handiwork, too. Militants scattered as their world descended into chaos.

It was glorious.

"Let's blow this shithole."

Her finger spasmed over the trigger of her weapon as Crane materialized next to her. She had completely missed his approach, which changed her glee over flattening this place into a scowl at being caught unawares.

"Let's. But I'm driving."

He had the nerve to tap her on the nose. "Nice try, squirrel, but this baby's mine."

While she stewed over the gesture and the odd—not so annoyed—reaction in her core, he beat her to the driver's side door.

Climbing into the passenger seat of the beat-up Toyota truck, Rogue wasn't about to accept defeat gracefully. She checked her gun before pointedly saying, "It's probably for the best. They might follow, and I'm the better shot."

She caught his snort of disbelief before he cranked the engine. Or rather, *tried* to crank the engine. They'd chosen this truck because of its proximity to the gate and the fact the keys had been conveniently left inside.

Now we know why.

As if he could will it to life, Crane kept trying. The vehicle responded with hopeless clicking.

She rolled her eyes and tugged at his arm. "Stop. The battery's dead."

When he turned to look at her, his pupils were wild with something that looked suspiciously close to panic before he growled, "It can't be. We blew everything else up."

Her eyes widened in surprise. Wow, the big guy was wigging out on her.

"Plan B, remember?" She flashed a grin, hoping to calm him down. Then she shoved him toward the door. "Let's go."

He gave a sharp nod, but his mouth still sat in a grim line. Ignoring it, she jumped out of the truck and ran toward the military Humvee they'd tagged earlier as their backup plan.

They'd left it because to really disable it would have taken more than the explosive power they had with their need to spread the fertilizer bombs around. Plus, the thing looked like it was on its last leg.

The desert paint job had flecked off in places, revealing the dull metal underneath, but it still sported a roof-mounted machine gun. If she had to guess, it had been an old U.S. Army Humvee, probably commandeered after Desert Storm.

This one had four-doors, and she headed for the front passenger side. She'd never driven a Humvee but knew Crane had during his days as a Marine. Before they'd started this op, he'd mentioned the tour he'd done in Iraq and how much he'd prefer not to return to the country.

She understood the sentiment. After the trip she'd had so far, she never wanted to come back.

The door opened with a howling squeak, making her wince. Even with their fertilizer bombs still exploding and the roar of the fires they'd caused, the noise seemed to echo like a sonar beam straight to their location.

"Hurry!" she hissed as Crane took stock of the dash. When the engine turned over, she demanded, "Can you drive this thing or what?"

Finally, his grin came back. It did strange things to her insides as he said, "Hold on," and hit the gas.

The ancient vehicle lurched forward, and she loosed a breath in relief. She'd spent more than enough time on this compound and wanted to put it in the rearview mirror. *Like yesterday.*

The exit gate loomed closer as they sped over the dry desert earth. Dust clouds signaled their movement, and it wouldn't be long before someone noticed, even in the dark. Swallowing down the ball of fear in her throat, Rogue focused on their egress route.

They would have to crash through the front gate, and she prayed the lock on it wouldn't hold. It didn't look *too* sturdy. The whole thing consisted of chain-link fencing bounded by metal supports that met in two squares on either side of the opening. The support bars extended about a foot above the main gate with coiled barbed wire wrapping the top. Which was great if you wanted to keep people from climbing it on foot, but it wouldn't do a damned thing to the Humvee—she hoped.

About to tell Crane to step on it to be sure, ominous pings lit up her side of the vehicle. Glancing out the dusty window, Rogue made out a militant firing on them. "Damn it! They've seen us."

"Fuck!" Crane cursed and pushed the pedal to the floor. "This thing's too old to be armored." It didn't seem to make much of a difference, though. The Humvee hadn't been built for speed.

The militants who'd been manning the guard shack by the gate ran after them, sending a barrage of bullets from assault rifles. At least their aim sucked.

"Who are these assholes?" she muttered the question under her breath. Whenever they made it back stateside, she had every intention of finding out. *And* making sure their gun dealings and whatever other pies they had their fingers in were a thing of the past.

Sometimes, it pays to know people.

* * *

Crane

Crane glanced over at Rogue in time to see a sinister smile tilt her lips up. "Do I want to know what you're thinking about over there?"

"Nope." She shook her head. "Just drive, big guy."

He grinned at the nickname. They weren't out of the woods yet, but at least the overwhelming fear had passed. After nearly petrifying him. Whether from the length of this operation or the high stakes, he was on edge way more than usual.

The thought of failing Rogue . . . it choked him, clouded his brain when he needed to be sharp. He'd always been good at thinking on his feet, but when the truck hadn't cranked, his mind had blanked and plunged right into panic.

Uncomfortable with the 'why' behind it, Crane's hands tightened on the wheel. They were almost to the gate, except . . .

"Why'd they stop shooting?" Worry crept into his tone as he glanced over at Rogue.

She reared up to check behind them, only to let out a slew of curses before plopping back in her seat. "They're giving chase on dirt bikes."

"Damn it! We missed those."

"Think we can outrun them?" Rogue asked, but her gaze stayed trained out the window.

In a brand-new Humvee? Possibly. In this old-ass junk of metal . . . "Probably not."

With another curse, she disappeared over the seat.

"What are you doing?" A hint of fear

tinged his question. He didn't like her being out of sight when they were still in danger.

He didn't miss the smirk in her voice when she said, "In case you hadn't noticed, this thing has an M60."

Instead of that fact being a relief, it shot his blood pressure through the roof. Not that he wouldn't love for her to fire at the militants and stop their pursuit, but it meant putting herself in danger to do so.

"Dammit, Rogue. What if they shoot back?" He reached blindly toward the hatch in the roof, hoping to catch her before she climbed up it.

She yelped when his hand closed around her leg. Something hit the floorboards, crashing and rolling. He thought it might be the ammo.

"Let go!" She tried shaking him off, but the gate loomed right in front of them.

Crane jerked her back into the seat before they crashed through it. "Hold on!"

The force of their impact sent the chain-link flying open, and metal clanged against metal. They broke free with a horrible screech when pieces of the gate clawed at the

Humvee as if in a desperate attempt to keep them from escaping.

When he glanced over to ensure Rogue wasn't injured, he found her rubbing at her chest. The Humvee didn't have airbags, and they'd both bounced pretty good. "You okay?"

Her response came as a glare before she rechecked their six.

Her anger didn't faze him. She would have been hurt a lot worse if she'd been halfway out of the vehicle when they'd crashed through the gate.

"They're still following us."

A disgruntled sigh moved Crane's chest; he knew what she was going to do. "Don't make yourself an easy target."

She scoffed at that. "I never do."

This time, he let her go when she climbed over the seat. If they had a tail, the only solution was to get rid of it. Or their elaborate escape would've been for naught. That fact didn't help ease the rock his gut had turned into. He hoped like hell those fuckers couldn't drive and shoot at the same time. One stray bullet and . . .

Crane stopped those thoughts in their tracks. Whatever the hell was going on with him, he'd examine later. Now, the priority had to be getting to safety. They couldn't exactly take the road, so he cut across the desert in the direction he knew as north—toward TOP's safehouse. The speedometer read 50 despite the pedal being all the way to the floor.

"Come on, baby. You've got more than this." He stroked the dash. "It's okay, you can show off for me."

Rogue heard his crooning because she didn't miss the chance to tease him. "Are you sweet-talking the Humvee?" Her chuckle tightened his stomach muscles as if she'd caressed him there. "I'm pretty sure it's a dude."

She hadn't started shooting yet, and he began to wonder if something was wrong with the equipment, but he said, "Doesn't mean he won't like being called 'baby.'"

She snorted, then let out a shout filled with disturbing glee. Clearly, whatever the hang-up had been, she'd fixed it. "Time to pay, assholes."

The rapid report of the machine gun drowned out the noise of the engine as Rogue aimed at the two dirt bikes following them. He didn't know how much ammo she had up there but hoped it would be enough.

Through the windshield, darkness encased them, split only by the tunnel carved from the Humvee's headlights. So when a flash from the side-view mirror drew his eye, Crane paid attention. The light proved too dim to see what had happened, but only a single beam bounced in the reflection. Rogue had gotten one.

Nice shooting, baby.

The unbidden use of the endearment made him frown. Since when did he call Rogue 'baby'? She'd probably slug him if he tried it out loud. Distracted, they hit a pothole, and her ass bounced into his face along with a stream of curses.

He gripped her right cheek, ostensibly to push her out of the way but really to take advantage of the unintentional opportunity to feel those curves.

"Dammit, Crane!" The shout came before she righted herself, smacking his hand away.

"I'm almost out of ammo. Keep it steady."

"Kind of hard to avoid potholes in the dark," he mumbled with a grin she couldn't see.

The sound of the machine gun firing sobered him up. He needed to focus on the task at hand, not think about what he wanted to do with Rogue's backside.

Down boy. Shifting in his seat, he willed his dick to behave. The relief-charged adrenaline filtering through his veins wasn't helping.

The militants' compound had been around eighty miles from Baghdad, which meant they could be to the safehouse outside Al Asad within a couple of hours. If they were lucky, the rest of the team would still be there.

Rogue dropped into the seat next to him with a satisfied gleam in her eyes. "Tangoes eliminated."

He smiled in response. They were one step closer to getting the hell out of this country. The rock in his gut felt lighter until his eye landed on another problem.

Staring at the reading on the dashboard,

it sank like a stone, heavy enough to drag all hope down with it.

With a glance at Rogue's profile, Crane uttered five words capable of turning their clean escape into an easy recapture. "We're running out of gas."

CHAPTER 5

Rogue

"I'm not in the mood for jokes." Even though Rogue wanted those words to be filled with exasperation, they came out hesitant. Because something in Crane's tone had told her he wasn't kidding.

They *were* running out of gas.

He didn't respond, but the rigid set of his jaw meant they were in trouble.

Swallowing down the dread rushing up her throat, she asked in a voice she hardly recognized, "How long?"

"At this rate?" His laugh lacked any humor. "Maybe we'll get a couple more miles."

Not good.

They hadn't gone nearly far enough away from the militants' camp to be comfortable. The fear she'd successfully battled all day threatened to overwhelm her when a fresh tide swamped her. Fighting against its tug, she clenched her hands into fists on her lap. "I won't go back there." Her quiet statement was both a promise and a plea.

Crane surprised her by reaching over to clasp her hand. "You won't."

Tingles of warmth radiated up her arm as she stared down at his large palm engulfing hers. He couldn't promise her that, but his voice had sounded so sure the words soothed some of the panic clawing at her.

In the light of the cab, she could see the skin around her wrists no longer looked so irritated. She preferred not to have them bound in rope again. When he squeezed her hand, the sweet gesture tempted her to turn her palm up and grasp his . . . but she didn't. Partly because she feared what it would mean and partly because they still had to work together.

When he didn't remove his hand, she looked up to find him watching her. An emotion swirled in his caramel eyes, which she didn't know how to interpret. Determination fired his gaze, but something else burned along with it—something softer, warmer.

Warm enough to make her insides jumpy.

Rogue jerked her head and her hand away. "What's our Plan B now?" The question came out breathy, making her frown. Since when did her lungs stop functioning correctly?

When he answered her, the rasp in Crane's voice sounded more pronounced. "Keep heading north. On foot."

This meant, in addition to worrying about the militants catching up with them, they'd also have to worry about poisonous snakes and scorpions as they walked across the desert. *Super.*

And only if they didn't run out of water first. They'd refilled the reservoir in Crane's vest before they'd left the militants' compound, but they hadn't expected to need it to last for days.

An overwhelming desire to scream at the top of her lungs pierced her chest, but they didn't have time for her to freak out. She had to remember the important things—she'd made it off the compound, and she wasn't alone.

Before she had time to think about it, she blurted, "Thank you for coming back for me." She didn't know where she'd be if he hadn't, and she'd never properly thanked him.

As if her statement had been a spark, the tension in the Humvee skyrocketed. She felt his eyes on her but refused to meet his gaze. "Rogue . . ."

When she didn't look at him, he sighed. "I'll always come back for you."

The soft statement punched through her defenses with the ease of an armor-piercing round. Off-kilter, her gaze jerked to his. But then the vehicle slowed to a halt, cutting off the charged moment.

"Fuck!" Crane slammed his hands on the wheel, making her jump.

Instinct had her reach for his arm, but then she thought better of it. Touching him wouldn't help her keep her distance, especially when electric heat seemed to rush through her body whenever they did. Softly, she said, "Time for a hike."

When Crane turned his head, the tortured expression on his face made her gasp out a breath. He shifted toward her. In the space of a blink, he had her head in his big hands, one of them tangling in the hair at the base of her neck. Then he lowered his forehead to hers.

She wasn't sure what happened, but his breathing was erratic, so she lifted a hand to his chest. "Are you okay?" she whispered. Under her fingers, his heart pounded like a drum tattoo.

His eyes were shut, and she tried desperately not to focus on how good his hands felt holding her. With his lips so close, the desire to kiss him made her own breathing shallow as she wondered what a real one with him would be like.

In response to her question, he gave a slight shake of his head but didn't release her. Not until his breathing slowed to its normal rhythm.

When he leaned back, his eyes held her still as his palms moved to cup her face. One thumb gently trailed across her cheek to her mouth. Then he ran the pad of his finger along her bottom lip.

Holy hell.

A bullet shot straight to her core and melted into liquid heat. She'd never wanted to be kissed so badly. Her hand on his chest squeezed the thin, wicking material of his shirt into a ball as her gaze fell to his mouth.

When Crane leaned in for the kiss this time, she didn't stop him. His mouth on hers pressed as gently as before, but she wanted more.

She must've made some sound in her throat because Crane's tongue traced the seam of her lips and then dipped inside. He tasted like salt, dust, and something all male. His musky flavor lit up her tastebuds, and her body responded in a way it never had before. Every cell came alive, vibrating with an intensity she didn't understand. Then, her pulse began to throb at the apex of her thighs.

She'd never been so turned on by a kiss.

Not that she had a wealth of experience, but this was usually the point where she'd get disappointed and pull away. Next, the excuses came. She happened to be busy studying, working, or walking her cat, even though she'd never owned a cat. All so she didn't have to go on another date and face the possibility of liking someone enough for them to hurt her.

But with Crane, she didn't want to pull away. She felt no disappointment with his lips moving against hers, only desire and a craving she didn't know how to satiate.

His tongue caressed hers while the warmth of his hands sent shivers down her neck. The pulsing in her core matched the beat of her heart until she became desperate to feel more of him. She shifted, tugging at his arms with the need to have his hands on her body, but at her movement, Crane broke the kiss.

"Baby, I don't want to hurt you." His palms still gripped her head as his thumb grazed her swollen lip.

The murmured words shocked her back to reality.

What am I doing?

Even if he'd only meant to spare her physical pain because of a busted lip, her brain raced toward the future and the possibility he could rip her heart out.

Because Crane had the ability to make her fall—hard.

Fear of the eventuality had her slamming the poor, neglected organ back into its cage as she untangled herself from him. "We should get moving, anyway."

Without waiting for a response, she hopped out of the Humvee into the complete blackness of the night. At that moment, she thought it felt as cold and bleak as her life.

* * *

Crane

Crane blinked and stared down at his hands, somehow surprised they weren't still holding Rogue.

What the fuck just happened?

The passenger-side door slammed, and his body jerked against the finality of the noise. It proved as effective as a slap. Wincing at the situation, he climbed from the Humvee and leaned against it.

How could she be so unaffected when

she'd altered his life with one kiss?

In silence, he stared at the sky and begged the stars for an answer. With no light pollution, they cluttered the dark expanse above his head. If he were anything other than practical, he'd have made a wish.

But Crane knew wishes only came true if you made them.

Though right now, he wished he could read Rogue's thoughts. His own still scrambled to make sense of their connection. Grumbling about it, he crossed his arms over his chest. It had been a long time since he'd had feelings for a woman, but even the love he'd shared with his high school sweetheart hadn't felt like this.

Like he would burn the world down if it meant she'd be safe.

A ripple of shock had him sinking further onto the Humvee. He'd had relationships since high school, but he'd always been able to set them aside when it was time to go to work.

Not with Rogue, she never left his thoughts.

After she'd been taken, it had all come to

a head for him. A part of him had known, even if he hadn't been ready to acknowledge it.

He was a goner.

One kiss from Rogue and his world had spun off its axis; the ground felt unsteady under his feet, and he didn't trust his balance. Yet she'd turned it off as easy as flipping a switch.

Did I imagine the way she responded?

Her sudden coldness had him questioning everything. His mind replayed the noises she'd been making and the way she'd kissed him back . . . *No way.* That shit had been real.

Confused more than angry, he pushed off the Humvee and called her name, "Rogue?"

"Over here."

He flicked on his flashlight and followed the sound of her voice. Finding her bent over with her ass in the air, he almost wept. His dick had gone soft but now stood to attention again. Shifting uncomfortably, he growled, "What are you doing?"

"Trying to look at the fuel tank, but I can't see a damn thing." Pulling her head from under the vehicle, she demanded, "Give me your light."

He frowned down at her but handed it over. As soon as it landed in her palm, she ducked back under the Humvee. He had to turn away from the temptation to grab her curves, but he heard ominous muttering emitting from her lips before she sighed loudly and stood up.

"The tank is completely empty." Handing him back the flashlight, she added, "I found a hole. Could've been there awhile or could've been from a ricochet."

Crane only nodded, unsure why she seemed so interested in figuring this out. The fact remained. They had no choice but to continue on foot . . . across the damn desert.

When the thought had panic creeping in again, he clenched his jaw and shook it off. He would keep her safe—no matter what. "It doesn't matter. Let's put some distance between us and the Humvee before those fucking militants find it."

Her face blanched, and he kicked himself for adding to her fear.

Great job, asshole.

She nodded, then tucked her bare arms inside his vest. For warmth or comfort, he didn't know. "Lead the way."

After what felt like hours but had probably only been thirty minutes, he opened his mouth to break the silent trek. "How you doing, squirrel?"

Ostensibly, to ensure she was still with him but really because he wanted to know why she'd pulled away—or more accurately—*how*.

How she could kiss him like her life depended on it one minute and completely ignore the spark between them the next.

"Must you call me that?" The tone of her voice told him she'd probably rolled her eyes with the question.

His brain answered he could call her a great many things. *Beautiful, baby* . . . mine. But he wasn't about to tell *her*. Not when she seemed determined to ignore the chemistry between them.

"Just making sure you're awake back there." His teasing smile fell as he tagged on, "We've got about eight hours until the sun rises." Even if they walked all night, reaching the safehouse on foot would still take them *two full days.*

Rogue was smart enough to figure it out on her own. He knew she didn't need him saying it out loud.

"Have you heard anything from your contact? Because now would be a good time for a lift." She tried to hide the nerves with sarcasm, but he was beginning to read her like a book.

The fact he could didn't bring him any satisfaction. Not when her stress only made his own harder to tamp down. If they managed to walk the whole way, it was doubtful the team would still be at the safehouse when they arrived.

He wished he could contact them, but TOP had a protocol; they'd have already trashed the burners used for this operation. And with the company's strict security rules, only their team lead, Victor, knew anyone's personal numbers.

Which left him and Rogue screwed.

Frowning at the burner phone he hadn't gotten rid of, Crane fired off a coded message to the contact who should've picked them up from the militants' compound. He'd known the ex-Kuwaiti military member since his first tour in Iraq with the Army. Dafi had shucked his uniform and his country in favor of the almighty dollar. Money talked, and the man had never let Crane down . . . until now.

The continued silence meant his contact might be *unable* to answer instead of *unwilling.*

Not happy with the realization, a weight settled on Crane's shoulders, heavy enough that they threatened to droop. Gritting his teeth, he told her, "Not yet."

They walked for another fifteen minutes without speaking, the Western Iraqi Desert stretching for miles on either side of them. In the dark, its vastness seemed to swallow any sound. The quiet unsettled him; it taunted— a stark reminder of how cut off they were. If other signs of life existed, he didn't hear them.

They were truly on their own.

After their kiss, he had several ideas of things he and Rogue could do alone in the dark; *this* wasn't one of them. An overwhelming desire to ask her about it hit him. "Can I ask you something?"

"You do realize that question makes no sense, right?" He could almost hear her head shake. "You want to ask me something, then ask."

But would she answer?

Only one way to find out.

He wished he could see her face but didn't think she'd appreciate him shining the flashlight in it. Though his gut trembled with nerves, he took a deep breath and blew it out. He didn't want to hand her his heart only to see it stomped all over.

Unconsciously, he ran a hand over his head before testing the waters. "Are you upset? About the kiss?"

"What?" Her sharp intake of breath didn't go unnoticed. "What do you mean?"

"You're not mad?" Fuck, his throat felt too tight. He swallowed to clear it. "That I kissed you?"

One second.

Two.

He started to think silence would be his only answer when she spoke.

"No."

"No?" Did that mean she liked it? That she'd be willing to do it again? His pulse jumped at the possibility. "So if I—"

Her hand on his shoulder pulled him to a stop. "Do you smell it?"

Turning, he beamed her with the light, and she covered her eyes. "Agh! Would you turn that off for a minute?"

"Sorry." He gave a sheepish grin she couldn't see as he clicked the off switch. "What is it?"

"Something cooking, maybe? I smell smoke." She brushed past him, asking, "Can you see anything?"

He would've turned the light back on, but she grabbed his hand and pointed. "There. See it?"

Following her direction, he could barely make out the light gray haze of smoke rising against the backdrop of the night sky. Something burned, which could be good or bad. They might find a camp of friendlies, or they might walk into hostile territory.

Either way, it made sense to investigate. Water was their most precious commodity, and the camp might have some they could acquire. "Yeah, I see it now."

When she would've tugged her hand free, he held on, lacing their fingers together. He felt her initial resistance, but she capitulated with a soft sigh. "Maybe they'll have food."

Her stomach growled; he knew she had to be starving. Who knew what those fuckers had given her when she'd been locked up. At least he'd eaten an MRE before attempting his rescue mission, but the energy from it had evaporated hours ago.

A primal urge spurred him on. If his woman was hungry, he'd find her some food.

With her capable hand encased in his, Crane gave it a squeeze. "Let's find out."

CHAPTER 6

Crane

"Ahl al-ard!" Twin gasps followed the exclamation before two little boys raced into the array of tents at the encampment, screaming the term over and over at the top of their lungs.

Crane wasn't certain, but he thought they'd called him a monster. It'd be comical if the situation were different. He slowly rose from where he'd been crouching behind a water trough carved out of a metal barrel. His stomach churned with unease, not knowing who the kids had gone to tattle to.

Somehow, he'd managed to let the boys sneak up on him. They'd been as silent as the shadows cast by the camp's sparse lighting, so much so that they could've put a spec-ops team to shame. At least, it was what Crane chose to tell himself. Their superior desert skills had allowed them to get the jump on him, *not* the fact that he'd been distracted by thoughts of Rogue.

They'd separated to conduct reconnaissance at the camp they'd found after following the signs of a fire. But being apart meant he couldn't stop worrying if she was okay.

"What the hell, Crane!" Rogue appeared at his side. She'd been surveilling the north side of the camp while he'd taken the south.

Not that she could see his face, but he winced as he turned. "The good news is, if there are kids here, it's probably not a militant camp."

She didn't say anything as they hovered on the edge of the temporary settlement, out of the stream of its light sources, though it seemed the people in it used only oil lamps or battery-operated lanterns. No electrical poles had made it out here.

He reached blindly for where he thought her hand would be and connected with the soft skin of her forearm. Giving it a squeeze, he said, "It's your call. If you want to pull chocks, I'm right behind you."

"Sheep are grazing to the north."

Her answer wasn't necessarily an answer, but he'd become accustomed to the way Rogue's brain worked. "You think they could be Bedouins?"

He felt her arm gesturing and turned to follow the movement before she huffed out a breath with a quiet warning. "I guess we'll find out."

The beams from several flashlights bobbed as the people carrying them drew nearer.

Crane kept his eyes trained on the lights while his hand inched toward the assault rifle he carried. He whispered, "You're sure?"

Rogue's reply came as a soft grumble, which made him grin despite the adrenaline tensing his muscles. "You owe me dinner."

They'd made a bet before they reached the camp. Whoever failed to find food had to cook dinner. Since he'd gotten them discovered . . . he'd give her that one.

The grin left his face as the search party

stopped a few feet away. Four men had come to investigate. He'd been able to make out as much before they flashed a light in his face, effectively blinding him.

When they shined their lights on Rogue, a collective stir passed among the men, which raised his blood pressure. Every muscle in his body went on high alert. He reached for his rifle as the man who seemed to be the leader spoke.

The words were Arabic, but Crane had trouble understanding them. The man either mixed several dialects together or spoke one Crane wasn't familiar with.

He managed to pick up on a few, though. *Gun. Woman. Danger.*

Hoping at least one of them spoke the dialect commonly used in the western part of the country, Crane tried his best to explain that they were travelers who'd been kidnapped by a group of militants. He left out most of the details but told them about the Humvee and needing to get to friends near Al Asad Airbase.

When Crane finished, the leader turned his head and spat before launching into a tirade about militants in the same dialect Crane had used.

Relief they could communicate settled some of the nerves in his gut as he listened to the man tell horror stories of how these militants were ruining his country. From claiming their land, stealing their herds, and even killing the heads of households, it wasn't a pretty picture.

Crane's grip had eased off his weapon until the leader asked about Rogue. They might share a common enemy, but the Bedouins' strict religious beliefs meant they didn't view an uncovered woman so kindly. The leader asked about her *ird*, and it took a couple of tries before Crane understood what the man meant. When he did . . . the MRE he'd eaten hours ago threatened to come back up.

They were asking if she was *pure*—chaste.

With her busted lip, he could see why they'd wonder. Blood pounded at his temples as scenarios played out in his head. Them thinking she was loose or at least compromised, and going after her, *or* if he managed to convince them she wasn't, her being separated from him to keep her *ird* intact. Neither option settled his stomach. Unwed men and women didn't exactly mix in their culture.

The only solution he could find . . . He swallowed and glanced in Rogue's direction, wishing another option existed because she wouldn't like the only guarantee she'd be left alone. Hoping the apology he tried to telepathically convey somehow reached her, he had to say it—to protect her.

Making sure he had the leader's attention, Crane answered, "She's my wife." He felt her body stiffen at his statement. Stepping a few inches in front of her, he sent a warning to the other men, who still murmured in the dialect he didn't understand.

He focused on the leader, who nodded before asking them to move further into the camp. Crane caught Rogue's eye in a silent question if they should follow. When she made the sign for 'affirmative,' beads of sweat broke out on his forehead.

While the thought of food and a place to lay their heads for the night had its appeal, he couldn't completely shake the fear these men wouldn't come after her. He stood frozen with indecision, his hands on the gun he carried.

The leader pointed at the rifle he'd stolen. In Arabic, the man made it very clear weapons weren't allowed in the camp.

Some honed sense from all the time they'd spent together told Crane Rogue was about to protest. To keep her from getting them in trouble, he agreed and held the assault rifle away from his body. He would still have his knife, and she'd wisely hidden the Glock.

The leader motioned toward the youngest man in their group—a teenager who looked too young to have such a haunted look when he took the rifle from Crane. It made him wonder what horrors the kid had seen. Maybe he was personally familiar with the loss of a head of household. Had he inherited the title from a father whose life had been taken prematurely?

With a command in the dialect Crane didn't understand, the leader addressed the young man, who disappeared in one direction with the weapon. Then he gestured for him and Rogue to follow in the other.

Fighting the stiffness in his shoulders, Crane trailed behind their group and hoped this move wouldn't prove a mistake.

An eerie quiet descended as they walked into the lighted area of the settlement. Six large, rectangular tents made a three-sided square around a central bonfire. Each white tent seemed to have two or three sections, he guessed, for different rooms. A relatively even amount of space, maybe around twenty paces, separated each "home" from the nearest neighbor. All of whom had come out to stare at the newcomers.

Shining in the light cast by the central fire, Rogue's hair garnered more interest. His skin felt stretched too tight and his fingers twitched with the desire to grasp his knife.

Knowing that move would likely not go over well, he tucked his hands into the hip pockets of his cargo pants to appear more relaxed. But he felt far from it as he sized up the people in the camp.

Compared to the Bedouin's clothing, he and Rogue were both underdressed. The men wore the traditional galabeya, a long robe-like garment with a high collar. Buttons started at the neck and fell in a line down the middle of the chest. Though they wore black clothing, red and white head scarves wrapped the top of the men's hair. But the women . . . black encased them from head to toe. Some wore thin dark scarves over their hair and faces, while a few wore a niqab, revealing only the aging skin around their eyes.

With her hair, face, and arms bare, the contrast Rogue made seemed massive. Enough that Crane didn't know if they should stay. He opened his mouth, ready to ask if they could trade for food, then get on the road when the leader pointed beyond the open side of the camp to a column of smoke.

While he explained dinner was almost ready, it occurred to Crane this was the same smoke Rogue had smelled. His mouth started to salivate as the leader described the poached sheep and vegetables they had been cooking all day under a bed of rice. Next to him, Rogue's stomach growled—loudly. One of the men chuckled in response. Then, the leader gestured for them to have a seat.

As he and Rogue sat on the ground, joining the circle the men had made around the fire, the tension gripping Crane slowly eased. They joked, laughed, and told stories, including him in their conversation about the meal and their way of life.

Before they all finished eating, the leader invited them to stay, informing him they'd have their own tent for the night. Thankfully, Rogue stayed silent.

Despite their severe views regarding women, the Bedouins had offered them hospitality where he'd expected none. It was enough to make Crane happy a pair of children had thwarted him. Well, that and the fact he'd be sharing a tent with Rogue.

* * *

Rogue

"Married, Crane?" On the question, a noise left Rogue's throat. It was half infuriated huff and half helpless groan when they entered the tent they'd be spending the night in— together.

The Bedouin's guest tent sat further away

from the rest. It consisted of a single room furnished with a double pallet of linens made from sheepskin. Rugs of varying bright colors boasting geometric designs completely covered the ground, while underneath them, the soft sand acted like a carpet pad.

In one corner, a basin of water sat on a tray with small washcloths for cleaning up. The only other items were stacks of colorful folded linens serving as nightstands on either side of the palleted bed. The makeshift tables held glowing lanterns, which bounced their shadows off the white tent walls, amplifying one glaring fact.

One bed.

Of course, the tent had only one freakin' bed.

Today had been one disaster after another, so she might've been resigned to that point, but her resignation remained buried under the growing anger twisting through her blood like a snake preparing to strike. It'd be pretty damn hard to avoid any semblance of intimacy with Crane when they were sharing such a small space for the night.

Maybe it's a good thing.

She shoved the unbidden thought away as soon as it rose. Her heart might want one thing, but she had to use her head. She'd let Crane speak for them because she understood enough about Bedouin culture to know they wouldn't want to hear from her. But when he'd claimed her as his wife . . . shock had been the only thing to keep her hackles from rising. And it had long since worn off.

Now, she let the anger build to mask the fear she didn't want to face. She didn't know what she'd do if he tried to kiss her again. A part of her desperately wanted him to, and it scared the hell out of her. Fueling her anger, she whirled on him, ready to give him the full brunt of her ire.

He stood in front of the closed flap with his arms crossed like a bouncer guarding a door. As if he thought she'd run out or something ridiculous.

A current that had nothing to do with her fury and everything to do with lust attempted to distract her. Because the only thing ridiculous was how his muscles stood out in sharp relief. With the fabric of his t-shirt stretched across his chest, his shoulders strained the material, and his biceps flexed with every breath.

The fact she noticed only added to the complicated stew of emotions brewing in her gut. She couldn't even rage at him the way she wanted to. Who knew if any of the Bedouins spoke English?

While she waited, a flash of what *couldn't* have been fear crossed his features before he covered it with a stoic expression. "Yes, married."

She scoffed at his complete non-answer. "I'm sorry, let me rephrase the question," she paused and took what she hoped would be a calming breath. "Why the hell did you say we were married?" Okay, the breath didn't help much, but at least she'd growled the words instead of screaming them like she'd wanted to.

He cocked a brow while she tried not to breathe fire. "To protect you." His tone sounded far too calm for her liking.

Rogue stared and tried to understand what she was missing. Usually, she *knew* things. Things just clicked for her, and whatever meanings were or weren't meant to be conveyed, she could read them. It was one of the reasons she excelled at her job. But watching Crane for any sign of further explanation left her frustrated when the answer continued to elude her.

Tears pricked at her eyes, and she blinked furiously until they were gone. She didn't cry *except* when she got frustrated. It annoyed the hell out of her, which colored her voice when she snapped, "What am I missing here?"

"They wanted to know if you were *pure*, Rogan." A flicker of something deadly broke through his stoicism before he snarled, "What do you think would've happened if they thought you weren't?"

At least she didn't need *that* spelled out. She'd had enough of fending off attackers for one day. Watching the muscles in his jaw work, she tried and failed to connect the rest of the dots. "But being married isn't being pure." Those damn tears wanted to break free as she struggled to comprehend his reasoning.

How does that protect me?

To her absolute shock, he exploded. Like a grenade being launched, Crane blew up in her face, and she didn't even have the wherewithal to stumble back a step.

In one jerky stride, his long legs had closed the distance between them, then he gripped the tactical vest and pulled her to her toes until they were nearly nose to nose. "If they knew you weren't a virgin and you were unmarried—" His face paled, and his eyes pinched with pain before he closed them briefly and shook his head. "If they think we're a couple, they won't touch you." His jaw clenched, and his teeth ground together loud enough for her to hear before he gritted out, "At least, they better not."

Oh God, oh God, oh God.

Halfway through his speech, she'd wished she could disappear in a puff of smoke. Complete and utter embarrassment burned through her, suffusing her skin with its heat until her face flamed as scarlet as a rose. She finally understood what he'd done, but he'd been wrong.

She *was* pure. And even if she didn't want

to explain it to him, her fucking body decided to give her away.

Crane's hands gentled, moving to cup her shoulders as he set her back on her feet. Confusion replaced the fierceness in his growl. "What is it?"

Rogue closed her eyes, praying this would all be a horrible dream when she opened them. She worked to control her breathing, but it didn't have the desired effect. Her pulse refused to slow. It continued its racing beat, flushing warmth through her veins and reddening her skin.

Crane's hands moved to grip her head. One tangled in her hair while the other brushed across her heated cheeks. When they stilled suddenly, dread dropped her stomach through the floor. "You're not . . .?" His question trailed off as if even thinking it was absurd.

With a cringe, she opened her eyes.

They gave her away because he released her so fast; she could've been a viper. Stumbling back a step with a dazed look on his face, he said in a low voice filled with disbelief, "You *are*."

Well, damn.

Now would be a good time for a sandworm to show up and swallow her.

CHAPTER 7

Crane

"You're a virgin." The shock had knocked him back a step, but something else flooded his system. A fierce streak of possessiveness followed by a wave of excitement sent his blood sprinting through his veins. Rogue would be his—only ever *his*.

But as soon as the desire made itself known, a latent realization stopped him in his tracks.

She's saving herself for marriage.

He hadn't thought she was religious, but surely that had to be the reason. Because there was no chance this gorgeous woman hadn't had opportunities.

While he waited, all the questions he'd

had over why she kept pulling away found answers. It settled something in his being, knowing the why behind her actions. The hurt he hadn't wanted to acknowledge drained away like sand through an hourglass.

Because she had his heart.

The moment she walked into his life, the whole of it belonged to her. For the last two years, it beat faster whenever she came near, craving her recognition, approval, and love.

Now, more than ever, he wanted to show her what they could be together. So much so that he had to fight the urge to touch her again.

"Rogue?" he probed when she hadn't said anything.

Her face still shined as red as he'd ever seen it, making the few freckles along the bridge of her nose pop. "Yes."

He hadn't meant to embarrass her and stumbled over an apology. "It's okay. A lot of people wait for marriage." *Not any I know, but . . . probably, a lot.* "I'm not going to judge you."

A strangled noise emitted from her throat

before she said, "I'm not saving myself for marriage, idiot."

Though it hadn't been used in jest, he let the 'idiot' go. If she wanted to push him away, she had another think coming. "Then why . . ." The words were out before he could stop them. If the goal had been to make her less embarrassed, he failed—miserably.

No way would she answer. Willing to change the subject, he opened his mouth. Anguish flashed in her eyes, and he stepped toward her without hesitation, ready to comfort her. She turned away, leaving him staring at her tense profile. Her hands fisted at her sides while her chest heaved with jerky breaths.

Whatever she was going through, he wanted to help her with it. When he would've reached for her, her quiet words stopped him. "I'm afraid."

His mind instantly jumped to the worst conclusion, and he growled before he could stop himself, "Who the fuck hurt you, squirrel?" A crimson haze veiled his vision, firing his blood with rage. Whoever the fucker was, he would pay.

I'll plant my fist into his nose until no woman ever wants to look at him again.

She faced him with a defeated sigh. "No one." Her lips twisted into a wan smile. "That's the point."

Confusion cooled his wrath as he tried to decipher what she meant. It must've shown on his face because she took pity on him and explained, "I'm so afraid of getting hurt I've never let anyone close enough to try."

A thread of loneliness weaved itself into her words. Hearing it, Crane said fuckit and wrapped his arms around her. He cradled her head to his shoulder and wondered what happened to make her so timid in this when she was a force to be reckoned with in everything else.

Her body relaxed, melting into his, and he tried not to think about how soft she felt pressed against his chest. How right. Everything with Rogue felt right . . . like they belonged together. If only she could see it.

When she sighed, his stomach muscles contracted with the desire to make her sigh in pleasure. He desperately wanted to give her that—watch her come apart in his arms.

"My father . . ."

The catch in her voice stalled his libido as his mind jumped to the worst-case scenario again. If she lifted her head, she'd see the murder promised on his face because he wanted to kill the man. If her father had abused her, he didn't deserve to live.

Dinner roiled like acid in his gut at the thought of anyone hurting this precious woman.

I have to know.

The question burned a trail up his throat, but he swallowed it down. He wouldn't force her to answer . . . not yet. She'd started to tell him; he'd give her the chance to finish. Breathing in to calm himself, he ran a hand through her hair, silently urging her to continue.

"My parents divorced when I was eleven. One day, he left and . . ." Her shoulders lifted in a shrug. "That was it. He abandoned both of us."

Crane's chest ached for the girl she'd been. He didn't understand how a father could leave his child. His dad would never have done that. He knew he was lucky when it came to family. His parents were still together, still in love, and apart from being overly nosy, he loved how much they cared about their children's lives. He came from a family of lawyers, and even though he was the black sheep, they respected his choices and loved him no matter what.

Wanting the same thing for Rogue, he squeezed her tight.

"I saw what it did to my mother. We loved him, and he left us without a second thought." She pushed against his chest, and he loosened his hold as her head tilted to meet his gaze. Her rum-colored eyes were dry, but sadness lurked among their facets like occlusions in a gem. "His leaving destroyed her, and I never wanted to go through that. Ever."

Crane had experienced many things in his thirty years; real heartache wasn't one of them. He'd loved his high school girlfriend, but after joining the military, they'd grown up and apart. The ending of their relationship had been amicable enough. They might not have parted as friends, but they'd both understood that what they'd had only existed in the past. He'd dated other women since, but none of them had made him wonder what their future would be like together.

The way he thought of Rogue now.

Whether she'd be willing to entertain the possibility when she'd remained so closed off until this moment was a different matter. The fear she'd admitted to stirred a need in him to help her overcome it, to be the one who could.

He hadn't missed her use of the past tense and hoped they stood a chance, even if it had been an unconscious choice. Because he wanted the opportunity to convince her otherwise. He would show her they could be worth the risk.

Holding her gaze, he leaned down and kissed her forehead, breathing in the spice of her sweat, which always made him think of cinnamon.

When he released her, he grazed her lip with his thumb. The cut in her bottom one no longer bled, but dried blood crusted around the swelling. "Let's clean this up."

* * *

Rogue

Rogue was perfectly capable of cleaning her own wounds, but she'd willingly submitted to Crane's ministrations. The man continued to surprise her. She figured she'd shocked him with her admission, but he hadn't made her feel foolish over it. If anything, the comfort and understanding he'd offered made her less self-conscious about her virginal state.

Her eyelids felt heavy as he tended to her cut, and not because she grew tired. His hand on her face, while he carefully swiped cool water over her lip and chin, shouldn't have been erotic, but every nerve ending in her body seemed to buzz with life as if it *were.*

Sitting on the bed with Crane crouched in front of her, she fought against the pull low in her belly while his rough, callused fingers stroked her skin so tenderly. It surprised her to see the liquid in the basin turn red since it felt like he barely touched her. Because he could be so gentle in this, she wondered how he would be in the sheets. It became difficult not to think about it when his mouth was close enough to hers that their breaths almost mingled.

What would sex with him be like?

Before she had a chance to ponder it, the Bedouin leader barged into their tent with a frantic shout and wildly waving arms. He spoke in such a rushed manner she had trouble understanding him.

Crane had surged to his feet, nearly spilling the basin of water. She pushed it out of the way as she stood and tried to understand what was being said. They fired words back and forth so quickly her head spun until one, in particular, landed on her ears and launched a shower of fear that drenched her body—militants.

"They're here?" She wasn't sure she'd asked the question aloud, but Crane reached for her hand.

"Almost. He's going to hide us." He thumbed a finger at the leader, but her legs had turned to jelly. She was getting really fucking tired of hiding.

"Come with me. Quickly." The Bedouin

leader lifted the tent flap and shooed them through it.

Crane's hand still held hers, and she gripped it tightly, hoping it'd solidify the muscles that had gone slack with dread.

Would this nightmare ever end?

When they'd exited the tent, they followed the Bedouin man across the open desert, heading away from the camp. They were completely exposed, and she began to wonder if he was leading them to their death.

Maybe he'd agreed to turn them over in exchange for amnesty against his tribe. If she was him and he did plan to turn them over to the militants, she'd do it away from the camp, too. Far enough from the families there, he wanted to protect.

"Where's he taking us?" she whispered to Crane as they trekked through the silent night.

"Trust me, squirrel." Crane squeezed her hand with the statement.

But that wasn't the issue. She trusted Crane. This Bedouin, however . . . the jury was still out.

After they'd walked about a hundred

paces, the leader suddenly stopped. He knelt and tugged at the dirt. Astonishment dropped her mouth open when it slid away. He'd grabbed a cloth she hadn't even noticed it was so well camouflaged. Its color blended perfectly with the ground around it.

Crane flashed his light at the spot the leader had uncovered, and she gulped. It was a spider hole, and she knew what the man wanted them to do.

Good thing she wasn't claustrophobic.

"Will you even fit?" She glanced at the width of Crane's shoulders and then back at the hole.

"Only one way to find out." With a grim look, he handed her the flashlight.

"Wait!" she squeaked as he sat and slung his legs into the opening. When he paused, giving her a questioning brow, she asked, "How deep is it?" Visions of him dropping down and breaking his legs assaulted her.

"Not too deep. There's a ladder."

She hadn't seen one, but she trusted him and nodded.

When his head disappeared below ground level, she had the strangest urge to pull him back out of there, which was silly since she had to follow him. Hiding in a hole was still a better alternative than being recaptured by the militants.

The leader drew her attention. "Hurry!"

The distant roar of a motor shattered the quiet. With no need for further urging, she wedged herself in the hole. Holding the flashlight in her teeth, she spotted the ladder rungs. *If* you could call them that. They'd been carved into the shaft, and grasping at the layers of packed sand, she used it to lower herself slowly under the earth. She'd barely gone two steps when she heard the Bedouin man slide the cloth back over the hole.

Taking as deep a breath as she could around the flashlight in her mouth, she tried to calm her racing heart.

You're not alone and you have a weapon.

The familiar weight of the Glock hiding under the vest she wore settled some of the nerves threatening to make her panic. Focusing on that, she continued to climb down until she felt Crane's hands at her waist and froze.

"I've got you." Before she could stop him, he'd lifted her, setting her on her feet with an ease that spoke of his strength.

It did something to her insides. Made them all warm and tingly. He didn't drop his hands, and his musky scent permeated the earthy smell of the tunnel. When she felt tempted to bend toward it, she practically spit the flashlight from her mouth, desperate to see their surroundings and put space—if there was any—between them.

The sand had given way to a layer of gravel. Below it, stacked hard clay and sedimentary rock. These surrounded them in the man-made tunnel where they stood.

"Oh." It was around six feet in height and wide enough for someone larger than Crane, even, to pass through.

He smiled. "Yeah. Not so bad."

She attempted to return it. "Right. Could've been worse." Honestly, she'd expected something cramped and barely big enough for both of them.

Expected or hoped?

She shook her head at the ridiculous thought. Like she wished they'd been forced to huddle together with barely enough space to breathe between them.

Had to be the stress. That or she was losing her damn mind. She shined the light down either direction of the tunnel, and each seemed to stretch endlessly. It wasn't a comforting realization. Not when it made her worry someone else might be using the tunnel.

"What did he say about it?" Though she spoke to Crane she leaned her back against the wall next to the ladder so that she could see if anyone approached from either side.

"It's an old forgotten tunnel from the '90s. Part of the network Saddam built to hide weapons from the U.N."

That answer heightened her anxiety instead of settling it. Her gut twisted into a complicated series of knots. "It's not forgotten if the Bedouins know about it." She pulled the gun from her vest and felt calmer with it in her hand. "What if the militants do, too?"

Crane settled against the wall next to her and reached for her hand. She didn't try to move away when he entwined their fingers.

"I'm betting they don't."

His soft words were an attempt to soothe, but . . . "What if—"

"Then we fight." He faced her, and her gaze locked on the reassurance in his. When his hand reached up and cupped her cheek, she found herself leaning into it. "I won't let them take you again, Rogue. I promise."

She was caught in the honey of his eyes and couldn't look away. Excitement flooded her system; their surroundings faded, leaving her earlier question nagging at her. What *would* sex with Crane be like?

She wanted to find out. That much she knew for certain. She'd been fooling herself into believing she felt content with being alone. But a part of her had always recognized the lie for what it was. Maybe she *could* have sex without getting attached, and it would fill the hollowness in her chest.

If she was going to try it with anyone . . . it would be Crane.

"Rogan . . ." His Adam's apple bobbed. "It's really hard not to kiss you when you look at me like that."

Her gaze fell to his mouth. His lips parted

slightly, and his breath caught. Remembering what his kiss had felt like, she wanted to experience that again.

But now wasn't the time.

She blinked and leaned away from him. Gesturing with the gun in her hand, she said, "You watch that side. I'll take this one." Then, she turned away and stared into the darkness while her thoughts whirled.

She wanted to have sex with Crane. Not now, obviously, but if they made it through this and were able to use that bed in the guest tent . . . her stomach jumped, and she settled a hand over it.

When would she get another opportunity like this? She'd moved past the point of caring they worked together. By the time they caught up to the rest of the team, who knew whether that would still be the case. At this rate, she'd likely lost her job with TOP. And even if they didn't dismiss her after the bungled operation, did she want to keep working on a team who'd left her to die?

The question unsettled her stomach. If she *did* leave TOP, this may well be the last time she saw Crane. Could she lay with him once and let it only be about achieving a release from the stigma attached to remaining innocent?

The last twenty-four hours had been too many close calls. She didn't want to die a virgin. Never having experienced sex. How pathetic would that be?

Sharing the bed could be her chance to, if not conquer her fear, at least face it because she was definitely attracted to him—very attracted. Her brain conjured the image of the muscles in his forearm flexing as he'd wrung out the cloth he'd used to wash her face. She'd nearly drooled over the prominent veins covered in dark hair, another testament to his strength. She wanted to see what the rest of his body looked like.

One night.

Then, they'd part ways when they made it out of this country. She wouldn't need to worry about sex becoming a relationship or the risks involved in forming an attachment.

He wouldn't get the chance to leave her.

There was just one problem . . . she didn't know how to *do* that—a one-night stand. She'd never tried to seduce a man before and hadn't ever cared to learn how.

"Let's sit." His voice startled her out of her thoughts. He didn't sound upset that she'd changed the subject as he reached for her hand. He gave it a squeeze, almost as if he understood what she hadn't been able to say. "Who knows how long we'll be here."

He tugged her to the ground with him, and they positioned their backs to one another, each facing an end of the tunnel. His felt so sturdy against hers that she relaxed. Knowing she could rely on him and that they protected each other settled her pulse. Adrenaline still kept her alert, but the edge of fear riding it had been knocked off.

Even while the earth started to tremble around them. With her weapon aimed into the darkness and Crane holding her free hand, Rogue prepared herself to fight. Because that rumble meant the militants were getting closer.

CHAPTER 8

Rogue

A swarm of locusts descended on her stomach, and she fought the urge to jump away from Crane. The reaction wouldn't aid her plan to seduce him.

They'd climbed out of the spider hole less than an hour after they climbed in. The Bedouin leader had been right. The militants didn't know about the tunnel. They'd torn through the camp, upending furniture and scattering objects in their search, but hadn't ventured near her and Crane's hiding place.

She could breathe easily again. At least, she had been able to until Crane brushed his thumb against her lip as they crouched on the rugs knee to knee. They'd just finished remaking the bed in the guest tent after the Bedouins turned down their offer to help put the camp to rights. She thought maybe they worried about any more interactions in case the militants returned. The thought of those assholes coming back was one she didn't want to linger on.

"It shouldn't scar." Crane's eyes narrowed on her cut, and she blinked his face into focus. "Thankfully, it looked worse than it is." Though his voice remained light, she didn't miss the anger underlying his words or simmering in the well of his gaze like embers sparking on coal.

At the mention of a scar, she stared at the one across his chin. Stubble covered his face, but it didn't grow where the scar marked his skin. Her fingers ached to trace the diagonal line.

Wondering why she'd never asked him about it, she murmured, "How'd you get this?" while she gave in to the urge to touch him, lifting her fingertip to outline the pale slash.

"I could lie and tell you it's from a bar fight . . ." A slow smile creased his cheeks, and her heart responded with a somersault. "But the truth is, my little sister gave it to me."

Rogue snorted out a laugh, but a hollowness echoed in her chest. She wondered what it would've been like to grow up with siblings in a household with two parents who loved you. After her dad had left them, her mom retreated into herself.

Shadows of the past flitted across her features. She had always thought her mother liked the distance because no matter what she did, Rogue still reminded her mom of the man who'd crushed her heart. With a sigh, she acknowledged the fact she and her mother were very different people. Now, they saw each other for obligatory holiday dinners, but that was it.

Pushing the longing away, she teased him, "Lose a fight?"

"Nothing so dignified." He sat back on his haunches with a head shake. "We were playing tag—in the house. I tripped over one of her dolls and managed to catch my face on the corner of the coffee table."

"Ouch." She winced in sympathy. "How old were you?"

"Eight. Ali was five, but she'd always been devious." Mock disgust colored his voice as he said, "I'm positive she littered the living room floor with toys on purpose to create an advantage."

Rogue couldn't help but smile, hearing him talk about his family. "You love her." It wasn't a question, but he nodded anyway.

"My brother, too, even though Barrett called me stitches for the next year."

"How many did it take?" Her finger retraced the mark, marveling at the smoothness compared to the scratchy stubble covering the rest of his chin. She'd felt the scruff when they'd kissed in the Humvee and the scrape of it had sent delicious shivers coursing under her skin. Would it feel like that against the delicate stretch of her nape? The sensitive expanse of her inner thighs?

"Six." He smirked, and she fought the flush, warming her face in response to her thoughts. "Enough to make me look badass."

Rogue's smile stretched automatically, imagining Crane as a boy who wanted to seem tough. "Did you impress all the girls?"

He didn't answer right away, and her smile faded when she noticed him staring at her mouth.

Is he going to kiss me again?

"Something like that," he mumbled and stood. As if looking for something to do, he grabbed the now empty basin and the soiled washcloth he'd used to clean her cut earlier. He set them down near the tent's door.

Disappointment clanged through her like a bell. She missed his closeness immediately and frowned after him. If she wanted to seduce him, she needed a plan of action. Taking stock of herself, she winced at the oversized vest. It had to go.

"Do you think they have a shower?" She posed the question to his back where he stood gazing out the tent.

He glanced over his shoulder at her as if he couldn't bear to face her full-on.

Did I do something wrong? So far, her seduction was off to a poor start.

"No, but I can get some fresh water."

A weighted blanket of relief settled some of her nerves. Getting clean would help with her confidence. "Thank you."

Crane nodded before taking the basin. He paused at the tent opening, and his eyes were troubled when they met hers. "Stay here." With a frown, he set down the bowl, closed the distance between them, and pulled the Glock from her vest to place it in her hand. With a gruff demand, he added, "Don't let anyone else come in."

Accepting the weapon, she pursed her lips; the expression on his face stopped the scathing remark she'd been ready to make. A war darkened his brow as if he didn't want to leave her alone but wanted to comply with her request.

Without questioning herself, she reached up and smoothed a hand across the tight lines on his forehead. "I'll be fine, Crane."

When he stepped closer, she tilted her head. The emotion swirling in his caramel-candy eyes held her captive. Rogue wasn't short, but his height meant he had to bend down to kiss her. Her breath caught in anticipation, then guttered out in disappointment when he placed a chaste kiss on her right cheekbone.

"I know." Despite the simple caress, his

eyes seared her with the promise of more before he retrieved the basin and left.

At the look, the swarm of locusts returned to her stomach.

You can do this, Rogan.

With shaky fingers, she worked to undo the vest while staring at the closed tent flap. They were both attracted to each other. If she could get him to kiss her again, surely sex would be a natural culmination.

In disgust, she scowled at the streaks of dirt along her arms. A shower might be out of the question, but she could at least lose her dirty clothes. She undressed but had either adjusted to the lower nighttime temperature or the tent created its own warmth because she didn't feel cold.

Knowing she'd have to wear them again tomorrow, she attempted to knock some of the dust from her tank top and pants. When they were as good as she could get them, she folded the garments and set them aside.

After a deep breath, she sat on the bed in her black sports bra and underwear while she waited for Crane to return. Alternately clenching and unclenching her hands against the nervous energy making them vibrate.

* * *

Crane

Trying to keep my hands off Rogue might be the death of me.

Crane rinsed the basin before filling a water jug from the trough he'd hidden behind earlier. He thought about pouring a full pitcher over his head to cool off, but the water wasn't cold enough to do any good.

What he needed was the coldest of cold showers. Though he didn't have high confidence, even that would work. Grumbling, he started to pace. His body had gone to war with his brain. The former wanted to seduce her—show her the many ways he could bring her pleasure—but when he wasn't thinking with his dick, he knew he had to give her time. A chance to adjust to the idea of a relationship with him because he wanted her heart as much as her body.

The only problem? Whenever he came in close proximity to her, he ached to kiss her.

Desire had never cut so sharply before and ignoring it might be the most challenging mission he'd ever undertaken.

He stopped wearing a rut in the sand and blew out a breath, which did nothing to loosen the pressure, squeezing his muscles. Hoisting the basin and water, he made his way back to their tent. It was going to be a very long night because his blood couldn't possibly get any hotter.

Crane halted as soon as he stepped inside.

I was wrong.

"Where are your clothes?" Desperation strained his voice to the point he barely recognized it.

With a deliberate head tilt, Rogue pointed to the neat pile she'd made on the floor. But he'd already taken it in. What he'd meant was, why the hell wasn't she wearing them?

Sweat that had nothing to do with the temperature beaded on his forehead. He swallowed but the lump in his throat didn't move. Was it possible she meant to kill him? Because prancing around in this getup would surely do it.

She'd always been hidden under loose-fitting clothing, but now all her assets were on full, mouth-watering display. His gaze traveled up the toned length of her delectable legs, passed over the swell of her shapely hips to the narrow line of her waist, and stalled on the curves of her heavy breasts, barely contained in the tight spandex material.

Look away, asshole.

But he couldn't.

"What?" Her graceful fingers traced the edges of her outfit, and his mouth salivated. "This is more than a swimsuit covers."

Seriously? What kind of swimsuit does she wear? He instantly pictured her in a string bikini and whimpered.

She *was* trying to kill him.

"Is that for me?" Rogue advanced, and he instinctively backed up a step, crashing into the tent flap, which had closed behind him. He bobbled the basin as he caught himself, and the liquid in the jug sloshed. The metal bowl landed on the carpets with a thud. She grabbed the pitcher before he managed to lose its contents. "What's with you?"

The look she threw at him spoke of puzzlement, but he had to wonder . . . how could she not know what she did to him? A frustrated growl left his chest, and he grabbed her before he had a chance to think about it. One hand cupped her perfect ass while the other pulled her lips to his.

He felt her initial surprise wane into acceptance. She opened for him with a little moan that triggered a landmine in his blood. The heat of the blast clouded everything out, except the desire to feel each soft bit of her pressed to every hard bit of him. His hands roamed her curves, but the damn jug got in the way. She still held it, wedged between their chests.

While he practically mauled her like some kind of rabid bear.

"Fuck, I'm sorry." Crane pushed her away and scrubbed both hands over his face, afraid to meet her gaze.

"Why? I want . . ." When she trailed off, he looked at her. Her cheeks had flushed with embarrassed heat.

"Tell me what you want, Rogue," he rasped with the last shred of his control.

"Because what *I want* is to make you come *over* and *over again*."

Her lips parted, releasing a shocked breath at the same time her hands slackened their hold on the jug of water. He snagged it from her before she dropped it and set it on the ground next to where the basin had fallen.

"Um," she mumbled.

Watching her teeth assault her lower lip while desire swirled in the dark rum of her eyes was sweet agony. The color in her cheeks flared again, and an invisible force pulled him closer until he breathed in the same air as her.

Even battle-worn, her sweetly spicy scent enticed him like no fancy perfume ever had. Savoring it, he leaned in further. Her skin felt as smooth as silk under the glide of his nose as he tested the heat blooming along her cheeks. "Whatever you want, Rogue. It's yours." *I'm yours.*

Though he didn't say the words aloud, their truth seared itself into the marrow of his bones—more permanent than any tattoo, which would only fade with time.

"I don't know how to do this." She let out a huff of disgust. "But I want to." Her hands gripped his shirt in tight fists. "I want you."

The part of him, which hadn't wanted to pressure her, evaporated into steam when his blood fired at her request. They would have the physical and so much more. His heart wouldn't settle for less.

Cupping her face, he kissed the line between her brows. "Then let me show you."

CHAPTER 9

Rogue

The heat in Crane's eyes was a solar flare capable of decimating her insides. Rogue tried to breathe through it, but her stomach had lodged itself in her chest cavity, stealing precious air from her lungs.

If he kept looking at her like that, she might spontaneously combust.

She'd demanded the use of the washbasin before they did anything, but it proved hard to focus on cleaning the dirt from her arms with his gaze trained on her every movement. He sat on the edge of the bed with his hands balled into fists in his pants pockets.

Clearing her throat, she asked, "Can you give me a minute?" To make sure he understood, she pointed toward the tent flap. She needed to wash some very important parts, and she couldn't do it with an audience.

His sigh was audible, but he stood to leave. "I'll be right outside."

"Great!" Oh God, her voice climbed several octaves as if she'd suddenly inhaled helium.

Way to sound like a nervous wreck!

He gave her a strange look but, thankfully, didn't comment. She wanted the cleansing ritual to give herself time to calm down, even at the risk of trying his patience.

When he disappeared through the flap, Rogue blew out a breath. She needed a drink or *something* to settle her nerves. She'd faced down armed men and not been *this* wound up.

As quickly as she could, she removed the rest of her clothes and scrubbed herself clean. But it didn't stop her head from spinning.

What if I do something wrong? What if I suck at it? What if—No!

She mentally slapped herself and shook

out her shoulders. Time to stop being neurotic over nothing. No matter how things went, it didn't really matter because this would only be a one-time event.

With that fact calming her at least a minuscule amount, she climbed under the bed covers and called for Crane to return.

A frown tugged at his lips when he stepped inside. "What are you doing?"

She wasn't sure how to answer, but he didn't seem to need one as he stalked to the bed. "Why are you hiding under the blankets?"

The question irked her. "I'm not hiding." She wasn't . . . was she?

"I want to see you." When he started to pull the covers down, she instinctively wanted to hold onto them.

After scolding herself for acting like a ninny, she sat up, letting him look his fill. A shiver racked her, but it had nothing to do with the air temperature.

The honey in his eyes glowed as he said, "You're fuckin' gorgeous."

She didn't pretend those words meant anything, but she couldn't deny that Crane's proximity amplified the magnetic energy between them, heating her from the inside out. What didn't incinerate under his gaze burned with an impossible pressure when he hadn't even touched her yet.

But she wanted him to.

Arching a brow, she goaded, "Are you planning to do more than look?"

"A lot more." A dangerous smile built and spread across his face, making her stomach respond with jitters as if she'd swallowed jumping beans.

She didn't know who reached for whom first, but she found herself being lifted off the bed as their lips melded together. Her legs dangled, so she wrapped them around Crane's waist. With his mouth on hers, every nerve ending in her body stood at attention. She felt each scrape of his pants against her thighs. When his metal belt buckle pressed against her center, its cool burn fired off new sensations until her whole body buzzed like a fuse waiting to go off.

Without disconnecting their mouths, Crane lowered them both until he sat on the bed with her straddling his lap.

His kiss was all-encompassing.

In the possessive slide of his tongue and the rough glide of his hands over her, she felt his longing—desire gone desperate from leaving it unquenched for so long. She accepted the need spilling out of him and answered with understanding and patience she didn't know she possessed. Because the same need surged within her.

No one had affected her like this before.

Only Crane.

It seemed almost as if she'd been waiting for him.

She didn't bother to wonder why the thought hadn't brought any fear with it. The more he kissed her, the more drugged she felt. Enough that she couldn't think straight in his embrace. Her body became merely a vessel for desire. When her core begged for friction, she instinctively rocked her hips against the bulge in Crane's lap.

He broke the kiss with a groan. "Damn, baby. That feels good."

Too far gone to care about his use of the diminutive, she repeated the movement of her hips. He buried his head in her neck. She ached for more—more friction to feed the pressure building within her. When his lips found a sensitive spot at the juncture of her collarbone, she cried out, arching against him.

"Mm, you like that, Rogue?" His tongue trailed across the tender spot before his mouth covered it, sucking with enough force to leave her gasping.

What is he doing to me?

Her nails clawed at his back when his head lowered, lavishing the same attention on her breasts. Pinpricks of pleasure arrowed through her, lighting her up like a firework. With a noise she didn't recognize, her head fell back, her hands instinctively moving to grip his broad shoulders.

Don't stop. Never stop.

She must've spoken the demand aloud because he chuckled, and the air leaving his lips tickled her sensitive skin. "Baby, we're just getting started."

Before she could comment, he shifted their position, lying down and pulling her hips forward until she straddled his face. "What are you—oh, oh, God."

Words failed her when his tongue traced her folds. Sparks of electricity skipped up her back. Noises she was positive she'd never made before burst from her lips as he feasted on her with his mouth. Tasting her, teasing her, until her hips moved in a dance she didn't realize she knew. She felt wild and free as she gave herself up to the demands of her body.

"That's it, baby, ride my face." His words were almost unintelligible. She'd gotten lost in a haze of pleasure stronger than any dust storm.

It blanketed her, smothered her, and filled her up past the point of bursting until she detonated. As her back arched in a rigid bow, a shocked cry spurted from her lips, and lights flickered behind her closed lids. Every bone in her body liquified.

If this was death, she welcomed it.

Drifting among the waves of pleasure, she melted into the bed, falling forward over Crane.

While she lay there, he shifted out from under her and spoke. But her ears were still roaring. She'd just had the most powerful orgasm of her life.

E-ver.

He'd blown away any expectations she'd had. Of course, she'd hoped sex with Crane would be good, but this didn't even exist in the same realm as good. It was fucking astronomical.

Shit. Did he ruin her for any other man?

* * *

Crane

"Are you still with me, squirrel?" He couldn't resist stroking his hand across the delicate ridges of her spine. All her smooth, tanned skin begged to be touched. He'd shifted out from under her and now lay propped on an elbow next to her prone form.

She groaned at his use of the nickname, making him grin. He'd figured it would get her moving, and he was right. She rolled over, blinking up at him.

"I don't think I can move."

A lance of pride and deep satisfaction coursed through him at her words, widening his grin. He'd made her feel this way. Him.

And no one else.

He brushed a few blonde strands off her face and teased, "You just did." Leaning in, he nipped the soft skin of her breast. Her gasp made him chuckle. "Besides, we're not finished yet." He pulled back to catch the eyes she'd narrowed at him.

"Pretty proud of yourself, aren't you?"

Tracing her collarbone with his finger, he lingered over the spot she'd seemed to like. "Are you suggesting I shouldn't be?"

"It's poor form to gloat." The twitch of her lips ruined the superior look she shot at him. Any second, the laugh he saw in her eyes would bubble out.

With a smirk, he tossed back, "You're welcome."

She tried to hide the giggle with a fake cough, but it didn't work. The battle was lost. Mirth shook her frame, and he had to smile at the happiness bursting out of her despite the nerves he'd sensed in her earlier. Finally, she'd relaxed.

The lamplight reflected in her eyes as he watched her, casting them with a golden glow. They were warm enough he wanted to sink into them. The thought caused a flutter in his chest. A new and strange sensation, as if seeing her like this, made his heart desperate to give itself to her.

She's not ready.

He scraped a hand over the spot near his sternum, rustling the material of his shirt and pushing the feeling away. There would be time to tell her how he felt—later. Right now, it would only scare her away.

When she had her laughter under control, she said, "I guess you're pretty good at that, big guy."

"You guess?" He clapped a hand to his chest in mock alarm as if she'd wounded him. "Apparently, I need to prove myself to you." He rolled so he hovered over her, a forearm braced on either side of her head.

As he grinned down at her, she nibbled her lip, and the nerves returned to her expression. Bending, Crane gently kissed her sore and told her, "We can stop here, Rogue. Whatever you want." He'd go as slow as she needed.

But she gave her head a slight shake. "No. I want this."

He read the truth in the plea swimming in her eyes and nodded. "Then let me love you."

The words were a slip of the tongue, but she wouldn't know how deeply he meant them. Tucking the overwhelming tide of emotions away, he placed his lips on hers in a kiss that started tender but heated much too quickly.

She triggered something in him—some primal instinct. Wild and savage, he strained against the desperate need to claim her and make her his.

Mine. Only mine.

His head screamed at him to slow down as they rolled across the bed, his hands determined to possess and take. Though the air in the tent remained a pleasant temperature, they created enough heat together to have sweat slickening their bodies. It made his clothing adhere like a second skin, but he didn't notice. His vision narrowed to Rogue's face, dewed with moisture as pleasure raced over her features while his hands and mouth worshiped her breasts.

She arched against him, and he released

her. Her breaths came in ragged puffs as she tugged at his shirt, her hands traveling over him on their quest to test and discover. Reaching between his shoulder blades, he grasped the material and pulled it over his head. When he tossed it away, Rogue turned them so that she straddled him, her busy hands racing over his skin.

"How do you look like this?" she murmured before bending and tracing his abs with her tongue. Barbs of pleasure made his muscles contract and his cock twitch in excitement. She clearly noticed because the smile she aimed at him spoke of pure feminine satisfaction. As if testing him, she gave his pectoral muscles the same attention.

With a groan, he pulled her head to his and captured her greedy mouth. If she kept teasing him like that, he'd lose the grip he had on his control. After waiting years to have her, he didn't want to rush things. She was giving him a gift, and he wanted to treasure it no matter what his body demanded.

But when he trailed a finger up her thigh

to her center, he found her wet and ready. A hum of pleasure rumbled through his chest before he broke their kiss. He wanted to see her face as he slid his finger into her heat.

She shivered when he entered her, but desire sparked in her eyes. They were as deep as a cup of black coffee and just as potent. His forehead reached for hers. "You're so tight."

Fresh sweat broke out on his face. She was so fucking tight. Too tight. He knew he'd hurt her and wanted to make sure he made the rest of it as good for her as he possibly could.

They might be hiding from reality, but he wanted to give her this fantasy. The militants—what would happen if they were found—even the Bedouins faded away until only Rogue existed. She could be queen of this desert and he a loyal soldier who'd gladly give his life for hers but who'd even more gladly share it with her.

Wiggling against his hand, she moaned, so he added a second finger, stretching her. Her head fell back on a gasp. "Crane!"

When he used his thumb on her sensitive

bud while he stroked her inner walls with his fingers, her hands slapped his chest, her gaze searing him with wonder and hunger so sharp it proved all he could do not to answer it with his own.

But he'd give her this first.

She whimpered, and he spurred her on, gripping her hip with his free hand and urging her to move. "Use my hand, baby. Make it feel good."

He reared up, catching one of her dark pink nipples in his mouth. She bucked against him but gripped his shoulders as she rocked into his palm. The noises she made, the little gasps and whimpers as she searched for the perfect spot, drove him mad with lust. He bit harder than he should've, then gently laved the bite with his tongue.

"Oh, God."

He stroked her faster.

"Crane. I'm going to—"

Her breath caught, and he knew she was at the crest.

"Crane!"

One of the tethers holding himself in check snapped, and he released her breast to demand, "Miles." Dazed, she shook her head, but he gripped her chin and pulled those doe eyes to his. "Call me by my name."

Her eyes widened before they closed with a cry of "Miles!" as she flew off the peak.

Hearing her use his given name shot fire through his veins straight to his groin. It was pleasure and pain. Though his body ached with the need to be inside her, he pulled her close. Her head fell to his shoulder, and he held her while she shuddered with the force of her orgasm.

When her breathing evened out, he tilted her head back, placing tender kisses on her face before finding those sweet, sweet lips with his own. Rogue tasted of forever, of promises whispered in the night, and truths spoken at the height of passion.

With a sigh, she molded herself to him in a surrender that was sexier than she knew. It might not be a confession of love, but she had feelings for him; he was positive.

Even if she wasn't ready to admit it.

She leaned back, running a hand over the stubble on his chin. "You're still wearing clothes." Her laugh sounded surprised, but it quickly broke off with her biting her lip as she stared at the bulge in his lap. "I want to see you."

Her hand cupped him through his pants, and he twitched in response. The grin she leveled at him looked deadly. Like she lapped everything up and stored it for later use. That analytical brain of hers memorizing, cataloging, and organizing.

When her fingers struggled with his tactical belt, he reached down and unsecured it. He let her unbutton his pants, but as soon as her fingers dipped inside, grazing the hair on his pelvis, he hissed out a breath and stood. The thought of her long, graceful fingers wrapped around his length threatened to snap his tenuous control. If he didn't want to hurt her, he had to keep the animal of his need on a leash.

Right now, it chomped at the bit.

She frowned up at him. "Did I do something you didn't like?"

A rough laugh exploded from his lips. "No." Crane scrubbed his hands down his face. When he met her gaze and saw the nerves tightening her expression again, he cursed. "Damn it, Rogue. I'm trying to—" He shook his head and met her eyes with the anguish he felt shining out of his. "I'm so fucking hard for you. I don't want to hurt you."

She walked to him. With a smile, which said she understood, she cupped his face. "Miles, I need you."

Hearing her say his name, softened the sharp edges of his desire. They stopped jabbing at him, and he buried his nose in her hair. Breathing in the sweet vanilla of her scent, he thought it must come from whatever shampoo she used.

"You won't hurt me," she whispered into his shoulder.

Crane pulled back when he felt her hands at his waist. Nothing but calm radiated from her eyes as he let her finish undressing him. Achingly slow, she lowered his briefs and cargo pants. When they pooled at his ankles, he kicked off his boots and stepped out of the clothing.

Shifting away, he let her drink him in. But watching her watch him sent his pulse racing at Mach speed. When she did more than look, her hands softly exploring, he bit back a groan. Though his heart hammered his ribcage, he kept his hands locked into fists at his side, afraid of what he'd do if he touched her.

Then, her fingers changed from testing traces to a firm grasp. Her hand wrapped his length, and he clenched his eyes and jaw shut. It was torture. Exquisite torture. When her grip moved up and down in a teasing circle, squeezing him, his eyes flew open. "Stop."

She jerked away at his demand, but he caught her, crushing his mouth to hers. The kiss had none of the gentleness he'd shown her thus far, only need. The harsh craving burned through him and branded itself on her lips.

I need to be inside her—now.

Unlocking his mouth from hers, Crane nudged her toward the bed. With a rasp, he said, "Lie down for me, baby."

When she did as he asked, he took a deep breath, still trying to hold the leash on his desire. Giving himself a minute, he stared down at her. The soft glow from the lanterns graced her flushed skin, danced across the stiff peaks of her nipples, and bounced off the light blonde of her hair. It almost looked like a halo surrounded her as she sprawled on the dark blankets.

Mine.

She was all his. The knowledge settled something in him, and he lowered to the bed, kissing his way up her thigh, her stomach, her breasts, until he covered her tempting body with his. Bracing an arm on either side of her head, he lined up at her entrance.

The nerves that had plagued her had gone. Brushing the strands of hair off her forehead, he stared down into her smiling face. "Kiss me. I stop thinking when you do."

Needing the connection as much as she did, he met her request, melding their mouths together. Then, like ripping off a bandage, he drove into her, pushing past her body's resistance as quickly as possible. She broke the kiss with a gasp of breath, and he stilled.

Waited.

With his heart in his throat.

She'd clenched her eyes tightly shut, and

her breathing rushed past her lips in rapid puffs. "Rogue." When she didn't respond, he begged, "Look at me, Rogan."

She'd tensed; her muscles gripped him so tightly it was almost agonizing, and he knew it only made the pain worse for her. "Relax, baby. Just breathe," he soothed while his body trembled with restraint. A tear slipped out when she opened her eyes, and he kissed it away.

"I'm okay." He heard no strain in her voice, only a hint of frustration. "I can do this."

She lifted her hips to take him in deeper, and his eyes wanted to roll back in his head.

Fuck, she feels amazing. But he didn't want to hurt her anymore.

Inspired, he rolled them until Rogue was on top. She made a noise in protest, but he held her up, grasping her hips as she kneeled over him. "You're in charge, Rogue."

While she stared down at him with her lips parted, he let her slide down his shaft. Cupping her cheek, he brushed his thumb across her injury, determined to cause her no more pain. He would let her set the pace and depth, so they only did what felt good for her.

With her palms pressed into his chest, she rocked up and down, back and forth, until she found what she liked. Watching her find her pleasure nearly sent him past the brink. His muscles quivered, but he held back, latching onto the ledge of his control with hands that shook.

Crane maintained his resolve to let her lead as long as he could, but when she quickened their pace to a frantic rhythm, which spoke of her release, the tether he'd had on his control finally snapped. Like a rubberband recoiling, it vibrated through him, stinging him with desperate strikes. Half wild, he sprang up and feasted on her breasts.

She moaned, and he grabbed her delectable ass, then gripped her hips and drove her in a frenzy. She was so hot and wet and tight. A thread of sanity breached the haze of his arousal when he felt her shudder under his tongue as her release rippled through her. With another pump of his hips, he chased her over the edge into oblivion.

Minutes ticked by in the silence of pleasurable stillness. Sweat slicked their bodies where their chests heaved and met with each breath.

Sated.

Exhausted.

Crane hugged her close and vowed never to let go.

I love you.

He wanted to give her the words, but for now, he would settle for showing her with his actions. Because Rogue was his. His everything, and he'd do whatever it took to get her home safe.

CHAPTER 10

Rogue

Rogue stirred from sleep with sweat beading on her neck. She was burning up. The main source of the warmth came from her back as if she'd fallen asleep with a heating pad on. She attempted to lift her arms and push off the covers, but a heavy weight wrapped her middle. Confused, she yawned and opened her eyes.

They'd turned off the lamps last night, but the rising sun lit the inside of the tent in a hazy yellow hue as its beams passed through the white fabric.

Crane.

She recognized the forearm holding her captive. The fact the bed was plenty big enough for both of them, but he'd decided to spoon with her made her smile. She could add cuddling to her list of firsts.

Sighing her contentment, she wiggled a hand free to play with the dark hair covering his skin. It felt so soft when everything else about him was so hard. Like the muscles hiding underneath the hair. The man was *built*. As far as lovers go, she'd lucked out with Crane.

In more ways than one.

Her cheeks heated as she replayed all they'd done together. He'd made her feel . . . powerful. She'd liked it. Maybe too much. Her stomach cramped with the familiar fear she attached to intimacy, but she shoved it away. Her resolve hadn't wavered.

One night.

It was all they would ever have, but at least it had been one for the record books. She snickered quietly as more memories bombarded her. Last night felt like a dream. If not for the soreness between her legs, she might not believe all he'd shown her. Or how gentle Crane had been. The man had a way of kissing her so sweetly it seemed like she became the center of his world.

As much as she enjoyed it, she'd felt like he'd been holding back until, at the end, she'd gotten a glimpse of the wildness he'd kept contained. A part of her wished she could've explored that side of him more, but their time together was done. Their one night had ended.

She'd let herself be vulnerable with him.

Her hand stilled on his arm as a frown creased her face. Speaking of vulnerability . . . he'd surprised her when he'd asked her to use his name. The request had felt strangely intimate—too personal. Like he'd let her in for more than sex.

Rogue worried her lip. Even if she didn't plan to get attached, what if *he* did? She would've groaned at her lack of foresight in that regard, but she feared waking him. Not only had he been so patient with her, but he'd helped her clean up and even held her after.

Would he have done that if he didn't care about me?

She wished she knew what his typical M.O. was when it came to sex because she was beginning to think she'd ventured into dangerous waters. Fake married was one thing, but if his protecting her meant more than simply helping a teammate out . . . *Was it why he'd been so overprotective? Why he'd panicked at the compound?*

She gulped against the acid burning its way up her throat. The dots were coming together, and she didn't like the picture they formed. But even as her preservation instinct rebelled against the idea, a part of her wondered what it would be like to be married to Crane for real. Would she wake up wrapped in his arms like this every day? Did she want to?

Yes.

Her mind and then her body responded in the affirmative, promptly seizing all the breath in her lungs. This time the fear couldn't be repressed. It wormed its way into her chest and squeezed off her air supply. Relationships weren't worth the risk, and no matter how much she might like Crane, protecting herself from heartbreak was more important.

With her lungs screaming, Rogue

extricated her limbs and her heart from his embrace. Despite their sticky skin, he didn't wake, and she breathed a sigh of relief. Thank God he was a heavy sleeper.

As quietly as she could, she donned her clothes. When she'd dressed, she fingered the stays on his tactical vest before putting it on. It was the closest thing she had to a shield of iron. She hoped, like the metal, it would dampen the pull between them. Let it protect her heart as much as her body.

With a lingering glance, she committed Crane's image to memory. The covers pooled at his waist, revealing the dimples on his lower abdomen. They tempted her as she dragged her gaze over his softly rising chest covered in sparse coal-colored curls to the strong jaw, relaxed in peaceful sleep.

Their journey wasn't over, but this felt like a goodbye. When the hollow in her chest widened, she ignored it. She'd made her choice for a reason, and she'd stand by it.

Outside, she found the camp already buzzing with activity. In the light of day, the little details she'd missed the night before stood out—the things marking this place as a home, like the hand-woven colorful strips of fabric decorating each tent. They flapped erratically when the wind gusted, catching her eye.

Most of the tents stood open, and inside, women appeared to be working on meal preparation. Several stares landed on Rogue as she moved into the central area where they'd eaten around the fire. The men she glimpsed quickly looked away, making her frown. They likely wouldn't speak to her, but a plan had formed on how to get out of there, and she needed answers.

Not wanting to wait for Crane, she headed for the woman in the closest tent. Maybe she acted cowardly, but she needed more time to replaster the wall around her heart before she faced him.

As she made her way over, sheep bleated in the distance, the sound and smell of the animals carried to her on a breeze. When she stopped at the woman's tent, the fresh cheese and cooked dough scents wafted through the open flap, replacing those earthy aromas with ones that made her mouth water.

While the woman peeled what looked like a potato to Rogue, she glanced around the tent. This one held a low table with containers, metal basins, and cooking utensils. More pans, oversized tubs, and bags of flour, she guessed, were stacked in another corner. No rugs on the floor here. They would be unnecessary in a kitchen, which this room seemed to be. In the center, where the woman kneeled, a fire pit smoked, waiting for the next dish. A platter filled with the bread and cheese she'd smelled sat next to it.

Would it be rude to ask for some?

The woman tilted her head to meet Rogue's gaze. She looked close to Rogue's age, her tawny features visible without a face covering. A thin black veil wrapped her hair and covered her ears, but it left her smile bare as she gestured for Rogue to sit.

Smiling in return, Rogue complied. The woman leaned forward and handed her a root vegetable—not a potato—and a small knife to peel it with. As she shifted back in her crouch, Rogue's eye caught sight of the bright dress the woman wore underneath the long black overcoat she had on. The red threading made Rogue wonder; black might be a requirement, but it seemed the Bedouin women still found ways to express themselves.

Using the dialect the leader had understood, she complimented the woman on the dress's color.

In response, a thoughtful frown creased her lips as she took in Rogue's attire. "You need dress?" Her stunted sentence suggested her grasp of the Western dialect wasn't as strong as the leader's they'd spoken with last night.

Before Rogue could respond, the woman stood. She'd gone halfway through a flap Rogue hadn't noticed, which must've connected to another part of the home, when Rogue stopped her, "Wait!"

The woman turned with a questioning look.

"I don't need a dress, thank you." But she did need something from her. Rogue begged the woman to come back to the fire with a hand gesture. When she returned to her spot, Rogue tried again. "I need a vehicle. So my husband and I can get to our friends. Can we trade for one?"

The woman's gaze assessed her for several long seconds, but the only thing she said was, "Peel."

Rogue did as requested and hoped the woman would have something more to say when she finished.

* * *

Crane

Crane jerked awake when the sound of an engine startled him from sleep. He instantly sat up, searching the tent for Rogue. His heart thundered in his chest when his eyes confirmed he was the only occupant. Throwing himself from the pallet, he pulled on his clothes in a haste to get out and search for her.

What if the militants had taken her again? What if she were hurt?

Panic built in his chest, and his thoughts sped through one horrible scenario after another.

How the hell could I have slept through her

leaving?

When he'd dressed, he crashed through the tent flap with the force of a raging bull, yelling her name repeatedly, "ROGUE! ROGUE!"

The sun glared so bright it nearly blinded him, and he didn't see her blonde hair anywhere. Children eating in front of one of the tents scattered inside as he ran through the camp like a maniac.

Where the fuck is she?

"ROGUE!" he shouted again as he shielded his eyes and turned a circle in the center of the tents. Light glinted off metal, and he tamped down the panic to pay more attention. A truck. Looking much like the one they'd attempted to drive off the militant's compound. The roar of the engine starting had woken him, and there, standing next to it, was a woman in a tactical vest.

His breathing slowed to a regular, if rapid, rhythm as he jogged over to her.

"Didn't you hear me calling you?" Crane resisted the urge to reach for her. To hold her and prove to himself she wasn't a mirage.

"What? No. Not over this noise." She

threw a hand toward the truck's engine, and he had to admit, it did sound unusually loud in the emptiness of the desert. But it didn't make him any less angry that she'd left without waking him. It mixed with the fear swilling around in his stomach, churning it into a nasty combination, making his next question much less calm.

"Why the fuck didn't you wake me?" he growled as his chest heaved. The Bedouin man and woman standing at the truck with Rogue moved several steps away at the aggressive signals his body sent; he had little care in his current state to worry about scaring them.

His tone had her whirling on him. *Good.* At least now he had her full attention. He was so fucking mad at the fear she'd caused him that he had an urge to bend her over his knee.

"Why does it matter?" The confusion on her face only made everything he felt worse.

She doesn't understand.

Her not knowing how he felt about her sliced at his heart. He squeezed the back of his neck with both hands and shook his head. For that, he only had himself to blame.

She'd already wounded him. It seemed only fair to tell her why.

"Because you have my heart, Rogan. I couldn't—" When his voice cracked, he scrubbed his hands down his face and met her wide eyes. "I can't stand the thought of anything happening to you."

"No, no, no, no." The muttered words fell like bombs from her lips. She shook her head when he gripped her shoulders, forcing her gaze to meet his. Panic swam in those intoxicating orbs. "I don't want it."

Another knife to his chest. He'd known she wasn't ready, but he hadn't realized her rejection would hurt so much. Dropping his hands with a sigh, which only hinted at his suffering, he told her, "But you have it anyway."

Her dark eyes snapped at him, then frosted over with an icy glare. "That's not fair. I didn't ask for it."

Fresh hurt ignited his anger, and he couldn't stop the outburst. "It's not a damn burden, Rogue!" He shook his head and then took a deep breath. "It's a gift." *How could she not see that?* Crane's jaw clenched and unclenched as he tried for calm. "And I'm not asking you for anything in return. I'm just telling you how I feel."

She moved further away from him as if afraid he'd try to touch her again. "I can't deal with this right now."

His heart lay bleeding in the dust, and she'd kicked a layer of sand over it.

Gritting his teeth, he forced out, "Fine."

"Fine." She turned and watched him from the corner of her eye as she pointed to the truck. "This is our ticket out of here."

And just like that, Rogue was back to the business at hand.

Well, if she could put it aside, he would too. With a strength he'd never had to call on, Crane pushed everything he was feeling into a Pelican case and locked it shut. Time to focus on his primary mission—getting her home safe.

"Great." His voice lacked enthusiasm, but having transportation other than their feet *was* good. It would be risky to stay in the camp any longer with the militants still hunting them.

She gestured to the Bedouins, who waited over ten feet away. "They rented it to bring vessels of water out here from a nearby town. I've been trying to strike a deal for us to borrow it, but you'll probably have better luck." Her lips twisted as she nodded toward the man he'd pegged as the leader last night. "He'd rather discuss it with *my husband* anyway."

Husband.

The word bounced off the case he'd built around his emotions. The wish that the word could be real didn't have a chance at penetrating the indestructible material. Plus, the case was already too full. He certainly didn't have any room left to care about her indignation over not being treated equally because she was a woman. Bedouin culture hadn't changed for thousands of years. And he didn't expect it to happen overnight.

Without looking at her, he managed to muster another, "Fine," before he went to secure their ride out of the camp. But as he walked away, the case securing his feelings cracked. Despite Rogue's rejection, hope still fought against the hurt she'd dealt him. Time might change her mind, so he'd give it to her.

CHAPTER 11

Rogue

During their two-hour drive out of the desert, Rogue tried and failed not to think about what Crane had said.

How he felt.

About her.

Every time her thoughts wandered in that direction, her heart beat against the bars of the cage she'd locked it in. But she did her best to ignore it. She trusted him to get them out of this hellhole alive, but did she trust him with her heart?

Unsure of the answer, she shoved the question away. No good would come of entertaining his feelings. Only heartbreak. She'd rather keep hers locked up than have him shatter it to pieces.

Wouldn't I?

A frown creased her forehead because a part of her seemed to disagree. Anger stirred in her blood, but it was directed at herself. She'd hurt him. The pain she'd inflicted had been evident in his eyes. Remembering twisted her insides. She hadn't meant to; she'd only wanted to protect herself.

But at what cost?

Glancing at his stiff profile, regret crept in, and she hid a wince. He'd opened himself up to her and she'd slammed the door in his face. A sigh whispered past her lips as she turned away to stare out the windshield. But the barren landscape only blurred in her vision.

Rogue's gaze remained inward, where something gnawed at her. A truth she didn't want to acknowledge. Instead, she chose anger. Anger had the power to override regret.

Because how dare he spring his feelings on her when their main focus needed to be getting out of Iraq in one piece!

Scowling now, she crossed her arms over

her chest, angling her body away from him to glare out the passenger-side window.

Why did I let him drive?

Driving would've at least kept her busy enough to stop from dwelling on . . . *things.* Like how she wanted him to kiss her again. To smile at her and tease her. *Anything* but the frosty silence she'd had since they'd driven away from the Bedouins.

"We're five minutes out." Crane's voice lacked the warmth she'd become so familiar with. The words were only the second time he'd spoken since they'd started the trip. The first had been to tell her about the message he'd finally received from his contact.

The man had warned Crane that TOP had left and requested he meet him at a new safehouse. Something about it had sent her gut spiraling, but she'd been too distracted by Crane's feelings for her to pay it much heed. Besides, it was probably nothing but her growing anxiety to get out of this country. If his contact could help, they needed to meet with him.

"Copy." Her one-word answer came out as cold as Crane's statement had been. She didn't even move to look at him. If this is how things would be between them now, she was more than ready to get home and part ways.

Liar.

Her scowl deepened as the inner voice she kept trying to ignore called her out. She never should have slept with him.

No. She should never have kissed him.

This is why she'd always avoided sex. Attachment was inevitable with intimacy. She *knew* that. Yet, she'd jettisoned all her reservations, anyway.

Stupid, Rogue.

Grumbling at herself, she sat up straighter and uncrossed her arms when the landscape changed. The arid, rocky desert gave way to a town. Streets started to branch off from the road they traveled. Buildings of different sizes cropped up along those streets, but they had one thing in common. They were all tan. Tan dirt on the ground, tan brick on the buildings . . . just *tan*. She was really starting to hate the color.

Crane made a left turn, and a large warehouse loomed before them—also tan. Though it did have a metal-shingled roof, which glinted under the puffy clouds moving across the hazy blue sky. Beyond the warehouse, a chain-link fence stretched around a runway. She knew they were close to Al Asad Airbase and wondered if this airport was a military or civilian one. Hope that they could fly home sparked in her chest.

"Is this it?" The question proved moot as Crane pulled into an empty dirt lot behind the warehouse. She'd asked it more to break the silence than anything.

He put the truck in park and killed the engine. "Yeah."

She thought it was all she'd get but then he finally looked at her.

"I don't suppose you'd stay here if I asked you to?" A hint of his usual teasing danced in his eyes.

As much as she didn't want it to, her damn heart responded to that look. But there was no way she'd stay in the truck. Raising an eyebrow, she tossed back, "Not a chance."

His exaggerated sigh loosened some of the tension between them. "I figured." He nodded toward the building and added, "At least, let me lead. Dafi doesn't know you're the package I went in to extract."

She could agree to that since the man was Crane's contact, not hers. "All right."

He offered his Glock with a slight grin. "Try not to shoot me, squirrel."

She palmed the gun with a smile, happy they were back on familiar footing. "No promises."

But he continued to stare at her. His grin faded, and then a shadow settled over his expression. It made her gulp as worry surged up her throat. She still wasn't ready to talk about what he'd told her. Even if she had his heart, she didn't know what to do with it.

Crane started to reach for her but quickly dropped his hand, his expression clearing. Turning for the door, he cleared his throat and said, "Go time."

Without another glance, he hopped out of the truck. Rogue frowned after him. A part of her had wanted him to say or ask something more. Despite the fact she'd told him to drop it for now. Was it normal to feel this confused? Because if this was what came with relationships, she was glad she'd always avoided them.

She'd grown accustomed to seeing a clear path through everything, but the longer she searched for one with Crane, the more muddled her vision became.

Why does this have to be so hard? Why can't I walk away?

Shaking her head against the questions she didn't have an answer to, she checked the Glock and followed him to the warehouse.

** * ***

Crane

The warehouse was unlocked.

An open padlock hung from the right-side handle of the double metal doors. They'd once been painted tan but now sported rusted hinges and bald spots where the coating had chipped away to the matte metal underneath.

If this were a safehouse, those should be secured.

Dafi wouldn't have been so careless.

Finding the warehouse open felt like an invitation . . . or a trap.

Crane gripped his Ka-Bar tighter, pausing outside the entrance until he felt Rogue at his back. His whole body vibrated with tension, not just because something was off. Having her with him, worrying about her safety, clawed at him. He'd tried and failed to shove the fear into a box.

"It's unlocked." Positioned at his side now, Rogue spoke barely louder than a whisper.

"Yeah." His agreement came out in a harsh puff of air.

Whether Dafi or someone else waited for them inside, they had little choice but to enter. The fact twisted in his gut until it became a snarl of knots. As much as he wanted to get Rogue home, he couldn't get them out without help. And without any way to contact the team at Tactical Operations & Protection . . . they had to take this risk.

"Stay behind me." He faced her with the barked command. One look at her dark eyes and his throat closed up. "Fuck! I don't like walking in blind."

"And you think I do?" Despite her biting remark, she looked the epitome of calm while he felt like a ticking bomb about to go off.

Adrenaline charged his system, and he couldn't stop the words that spewed from his mouth. If this was going to be it, he had to at least try. Because if he went down, it would be fighting.

With his free hand, he cupped her face. Her pupils widened in surprise; she looked like she wanted to pull away, but he held her steady. "Let me have your heart, Rogan. I'll guard it as fiercely as you." The words came out as a demand, not a plea, but her rum-colored eyes softened.

Because they did, he pushed, "If you give it to me, I promise to cherish it." Leaning down, he breathed in her sweetly spicy scent before placing a soft kiss on her lips. When she didn't pull away or try to knee him in the balls, he added in a murmur, "And you can put all the energy you use protecting it toward something else . . . like loving me back."

Her breathing hitched before she retreated a step. But he wouldn't let her run away this time. Capturing her chin, he laid himself bare. "I love you, Rogue. If we don't make it out of this—"

She made a strangled sound.

"—I need you to know that."

A thundercloud of emotions flashed in her eyes before they filled with unshed tears, and she jerked her face away. "We're not dying here, Crane. We've come too far for this to be the end." With the fierceness of a lioness, she gripped the gun and nodded toward the warehouse. "Now, open the damned door."

All business again. He wanted to push the issue, but it wasn't the time. A grim sort of fog fell over him, and he shut down anything that didn't relate to keeping them alive. Whatever he did or didn't feel would have to wait.

Bracing his shoulder against the left-side door, he signaled Rogue to move behind him and slung open the right one. When nothing exploded or whistled past his head, he took a deep breath and swept inside with her on his heels.

The building was laid out like a large open bay.

An empty bay.

It smelled of stale air and old paper. Sunlight streamed in from windows near the ceiling. Their beams permeated the gloom of abandonment apparent in the inches-deep layer of dirt coating the cement floor. Nothing moved except the dust motes dancing in the rays of sunlight as they passed through the metal braces supporting the roof. It was also deadly quiet. Until he took a step and the scratch of his boots in the dirt seemed to reverberate off the cinder block walls.

He paused and felt Rogue at his back. She'd moved with him but now they both stood stock still—waiting.

Too quiet.

It made his skin taut with unease. If Dafi had set him up . . . Crane didn't like where the thought led. He moved further into the warehouse, keeping his ears piqued for any other sounds.

Skirting the streams of light, he led Rogue to the shadows on the left side of the building. As he gripped his knife tighter than necessary, he marched them through the length of the bay. Determined to root out anyone who might be hiding.

When they reached the corner of the room, Crane turned and checked behind them. Still no movement and no noises other than his own harsh breathing. Rogue seemed to have melted into the darkness at his back as silent as any skilled predator. Speaking of, there weren't even any animals here. No telltale sounds of rats or other critters.

Where is Dafi?

Rogue tapped his shoulder, and he turned to see her signaling toward another pair of double doors. This set looked almost rust-colored with two large industrial pull handles. Again, no locks. They hadn't traveled the full length of the building, so Crane knew those to be interior doors. But what exactly lay beyond them?

He felt like a mouse being funneled through a maze. No doubt, some manner of foul-smelling cheese waited at the end.

"I don't like this," he growled low and shook his head at Rogue.

"Me either." She huffed impatiently. "But

what choice do we have?"

Oh, they had a choice. They could leave. It might not get them home but at least it wouldn't get them killed.

She clearly wasn't on board with the idea because she pressed her shoulder into the left-side door and motioned for him to do the same with the right. The flatbread they'd eaten this morning became a solid stone in his gut. He didn't think his body could be more on edge. Despite that, he did as she requested.

When their postures mirrored each other, both gripping the door with a free hand, Rogue gave a nod. Though every instinct Crane had warned against it, he pulled when she did. Unwilling to let her face this alone.

The doors creaked so loudly there was zero chance their presence hadn't been noted. Because of that, he nearly yelled at Rogue to stay put, but the hand signal he sent her did the trick. They flattened themselves against the opened doors and waited. Whoever had lured him here could come to them.

Breathing hard against his rising panic,

he kept his eyes trained on Rogue, praying she didn't go through the doorway. She watched him just as closely, though her expression conveyed impatience.

But it didn't take long for a voice to pierce the stillness.

CHAPTER 12

Rogue

"Crane, I was hoping you'd come back empty-handed." A man's voice floated through the open doors.

A voice she recognized.

Jordan.

She knew it wasn't the guy's real name. He had many aliases, and this was merely the one he used for TOP. In her time with military intelligence, she'd known operatives like Jordan and had never trusted them.

You pretend to be someone else too long, you forget who you are.

Crane visibly relaxed; she didn't share his relief. They might not have walked into an ambush, but she didn't trust Jordy. Well, maybe Crane didn't either since he made no move to enter the next room. "Where's everyone else?" he called out.

Jordan's voice grew louder; he must've moved closer. "Gone home. Like you were supposed to."

Rogue remained silent. She could only guess what Jordan was up to, but she'd bet 100,000 Iraqi dinars it didn't bode well for them.

Crane, at least, seemed cautious enough not to move into the open. "Well, obviously, you didn't either."

"No." She heard shuffling as if Jordan had moved something bulky. "Are you two going to come in? I have something you might be interested in."

Oh, she bet he did. And surely whatever it was would be deadly. Her grip twitched on the Glock, and she ran her trigger finger over the metal of the slide in an unconscious gesture meant to soothe her unease as she tried to determine the direction his voice carried from.

"Why are you still here?" *Good, Crane.* Keep him talking. She strained her hearing, and more shuffling reached her ears. Did it come from their right?

"I had a job to finish."

With the comment, she became almost positive he stood to their right inside the next room. She barely resisted the urge to peek past the doorframe.

"What the hell are you talking about?" The big guy was getting frustrated. She glanced at him. The resolve in his eyes told her he meant to face Jordan regardless of the man's intentions.

Fear for his safety cramped her stomach, and she couldn't stop the desperate plea. "Crane..."

He gave her a sharp look, but Jordan spoke, "You always were a smart one."

She could hear the smile in his voice; picturing it made her skin creep with an invasion of ants.

"What the fuck, Jordy?" Anger, confusion, or a mixture of both forced Crane to move. As soon as he cleared his door, her feet compelled her to follow. Self-preservation didn't enter her mind, only a certainty that she wouldn't let Jordan hurt Crane if she could help it. She still wore a bulletproof vest; he didn't.

They'd entered another open bay, but old furniture littered this one. Ancient metal desks, old military chairs with cracked leather, and three-drawer filing cabinets scattered the floor. Some toppled on their side, others set at strange angles like the wind had transformed into a whirling dervish and whipped through the room.

The same roofline windows let in more sunlight, which shone on Jordan. His dark hair curled under his ears while his piercing black eyes seemed as slippery as a wet fish. He stood next to a chair holding a hooded person. The figure's posture suggested they were either dead or unconscious. The only thing keeping them upright in the chair was the ropes binding them to it. Black rappelling line wrapped the person's chest and legs, securing them to the chair's frame while their head drooped at an angle.

"Who's that?" Crane crept forward as he asked his question.

"The op was doomed from the start. Those militants knew we were coming. But I figured they'd be willing to make a deal." Jordan grinned and gestured to his hostage. "I get the traitor, and they get a pretty prize." His eyes cut to Rogue on those words, and the puzzle pieces clicked into place for her. Contemptuous heat roiled in her belly.

This fucking asshole!

Her finger strayed to the trigger of the gun she held at her side. He'd given her up on purpose. For money, probably.

Her breathing accelerated with her rising anger. Jordan was the reason she'd been captured, beaten, and nearly assaulted. The hell she'd endured made her vision narrow to the spot over his heart. She wanted to aim at it. Pull the trigger and allow her bullet to tear through the flesh of this coward's vital organ.

"TOP still completes the mission, and we get rid of your little distraction there." As if Crane needed the added explanation, the asshole waved his gun at her. "It was a win-win. Until you screwed it all up."

She'd been so focused on her own anger she hadn't realized how rigid Crane had become beside her. With deadly calm, he stated, "You're the reason Dafi left me high and dry."

"I paid him a higher price, amigo." Jordan shrugged. "I hope she was worth it because now you're both casualties." He tsked as if he actually regretted that fact; she seriously doubted it. "Caught in the crossfire when I retrieved the package. Unfortunate, but an acceptable loss for the mission."

He raised his pistol and pointed it at her head. Jordan had been the mouthpiece for her naysayers at TOP. Constantly pushing to get her kicked off the team, but she'd never thought him capable of this.

The double-cross cut deeper than she would've liked. Mostly because she hadn't seen it coming. Too many successful ops together had left her complacent. He'd been a thorn in her side but hardly a poisonous one, or so she'd thought.

"Before you get any ideas, sweetheart, strip the gun and toss it."

Jordan wanted her to disassemble the Glock but as her only weapon . . . *Fat chance, asshole.* "And if I don't?"

"I shoot Crane first, though I preferred having him watch *you* die." The gleam in

Jordan's eye sent shivers down her back.

Not for herself. For Crane, who vibrated beside her. She could almost feel his body tremble with the effort it took to suppress his rage.

"You do that, and I shoot your traitor." Rogue lifted her gun and trained it on the slumped man. Her threat wasn't a bluff. She would do whatever it took to get her and Crane out of this situation.

Jordan glanced at the hooded man with a beleaguered sigh. "Our orders were to bring him back alive, but . . . a dead body is better than *no* body." The smile on his face could only be described as lethal. The promise it contained wasn't lost on her.

Her thoughts raced as fresh sweat broke out at her temples. It would be difficult to outreason him. She glanced at Crane, but his gaze stayed focused on the threat. Fingers of fear started to claw at her lungs. When her hand shook, she changed her grip, bringing her other palm up to steady the Glock. She shifted her target, training her sight on Jordan with her finger poised against the trigger. Ready for any chance to break it and fire the bullet that would end this. But could she manage it fast enough without Crane becoming a casualty?

Because she wasn't sure, she tried to stall for time. "There's no way you walk away from this clean. TOP already knows you sold me out."

His smile hinted he didn't believe her. "If that's true, where are they?"

She pulled answers from thin air, hoping a real solution might present itself. "They're waiting for you. Right outside these walls. If Crane and I don't walk out those doors, you better believe you won't either." She managed to come off as smug and hoped it made the lie convincing.

Out of the corner of her eye, something moved. She glanced over to see the blade of Crane's Ka-Bar flying through the air. Jordan, who'd been watching her, tracked her shift in focus and dodged the knife just in time. It wedged itself in a beam beyond his head.

With a coolness the situation didn't warrant, the deranged asshole smiled and said, "Thank you for relinquishing your other weapon."

Crane snarled and clenched his hands into fists. Silently, she cursed at him for doing something so stupid.

Jordan nodded at her gun. "Strip it, or the hulking birdman here will be sporting bullet holes."

For the first time in years, Rogue felt stuck. She didn't know what to do. Shoot Jordan and he'd shoot Crane, unless . . . a wild idea, but an idea, nonetheless, went off like a blazing lightbulb. "I'm sorry, Crane," she murmured. Though her attention appeared to be on him, her aim didn't waiver from Jordan.

As expected, Crane's head whipped toward her, his caramel eyes questioning. They went from confused to fearful in the space of a blink as he realized she meant to fire on Jordan. But before she had the chance to step in front of him and take her shot, Jordan used his weapon.

"No-o-o-o-o-oo!" Everything moved in slow motion, even her yell. Her finger squeezed the trigger, firing at Jordan as Crane's hands lifted to his right side.

When he staggered back a step, she moved to catch him, but they both crashed to the floor under his weight. He landed half on top of her. She sat up with a grunt and cradled him in her arms.

"Oh God, Crane." Blood gushed from his abdominal wound. On instinct, she lifted her hands to put pressure on the spot, but she still held the Glock. She shifted her gaze to Jordan. He was down for the count. She didn't need her weapon any longer. Setting it aside, she grabbed Crane's big mitt and used it to cover the hole in his gut.

"Jordy—" He lifted his head, and his face contorted in pain, making her wince in sympathy.

One of her bullets had gone through Jordan's left eye, the other through the center of his forehead. "No longer an issue."

"Good." Crane tried to smile at her; she saw the struggle in his eyes, but it ended with a grimace before his head flopped backward. "I'm sorry, squirrel."

"Why are *you* apologizing?" Frustrated tears pricked at her eyes. How had she let this happen? Her thoughts circled each other in a frantic rhythm, running through all the ways she could've acted to avoid this outcome.

It's my fault.

"I failed. I was supposed to get you home, but—"

His words snapped her out of the spiral of guilt she'd fallen into. "Don't say it!" She couldn't bear to hear him give up on her. "You still can!"

His eyes closed despite her desperate assurance. "I'm sorry."

Fear choked her, and she gasped, "Don't you fucking die on me, Crane. Don't you do it!"

But his hand slid away from his side to lay limply on the floor beside him. A strangled cry tore from her lips as she covered the wound with her own palms. Despite the pressure she placed over the spot, warm blood continued to seep through her fingertips. She felt it but she didn't see it. Tears dripped down her face and blurred her vision.

Don't die. Don't die. Don't die.

The chant sounded over and over in her

head while her body shook, her breaths coming as choked gasps of air. Everything seemed to shudder with violent tremors from her hands to her lungs as one thing became starkly apparent.

She'd fallen in love with him.

Crane's love for her was like a beacon, guiding her out of the dark and into a world filled with that love and all its possibilities. It had always been there; she'd just been too stubborn to see it.

Rogue didn't know when she'd fallen exactly or if people even knew that, but she did know this fact.

If he died, her heart would die with him.

Fear crept in and began to strangle any speck of hope. She'd never be the same now that she'd felt his love.

If she lost him, the crater it would carve into her heart could never be filled. As if in agreement, an unbearable pain pierced her chest, making her whimper.

She'd not only failed Crane, but she'd failed at protecting her heart. It was his. And there was no way it would survive this kind of loss. She had worried about being abandoned again. That Crane would leave like her father had, but this kind of leaving would be far too permanent. Overcome, a sob racked her. Rogue closed her eyes and begged for someone, anyone, to keep Crane alive.

Please. Please, help me. Please!

If he made it, she'd give him what he wanted—what she wanted, too. A life together. No more distance. No walls. She'd bare her soul for him, the same way he'd offered himself to her. Because she would risk her heart breaking if it meant there was a chance she and Crane could get the happy ever after her parents hadn't.

With him, she could have the family she'd missed out on growing up. Maybe his love could even heal the wound of her past.

Opening her eyes, she stared down at his face. Though slack, it carried the same sense of strength she'd always found attractive. "I love you, Crane." Her voice broke on the admission, but she added, "Please don't leave me."

The powerful noise of multiple windows smashing simultaneously made Rogue's gaze jerk to the ceiling.

What the hell?

She ducked her head and leaned forward over Crane as shattered glass fell from the sky. Shards clinked against each other as they bounced to the cement floor.

When the cacophony ended, she dared to lift her gaze. What she saw made her lightheaded with relief.

TOP.

Somehow, the team was here.

* * *

Crane

Rogue's head lay in the crook of Crane's arm where they cuddled together in bed. Her cinnamon and vanilla scent surrounded him, making him smile. He'd rather be no place else, even if he wasn't sure what he'd done to get her here. Stroking his hand down her arm in a lazy caress, he mimicked the way her fingers combed through the curls on his bare chest.

Leaning in, he kissed the tip of her nose, and those rum-colored eyes he loved met his with a smile. "It's time to wake up, big guy."

Her comment sent a bolt of confusion coursing through him. "I am awake."

"Wake up, Crane." Her voice grew more insistent, making him frown.

A beeping noise erupted, and while he searched for its source, she faded away before his eyes. "NO!"

"Crane! Wake up!"

His eyes popped open to find the latticed tile ceiling of a sterile room.

Hospital?

"Crane!" The strain in Rogue's voice pulled his gaze toward her. She stood by his bed, looking tired, her eyes sporting faint circles underneath.

Slower than usual, his brain registered his surroundings. The beeping came from the heart monitor next to him, but he didn't care about that. What his thoughts grabbed ahold of—what he latched onto with desperate fingers of hope—was the fact Rogue held his hand.

When she squeezed it, he blinked and said, "Hi."

A laugh burst from her lips, making him

smile, but it cut off too quickly. "You come back from the dead, and that's what you say? Hi?"

Dead?

But even as he wondered, recollections dive-bombed him. Almost faster than he could keep up with. The last thing he remembered was bleeding out in her arms. Crane winced at *that* memory. "What did I miss?"

She started to free his hand, but he held on. Her gaze fell to their entwined fingers, and he expected her to make some form of protest. Instead, a small smile creased the corner of her mouth. "A lot."

He tapped the bed next to his left hip with his free hand. "Then sit and tell me."

Worry pinched her face, creating a line between her brows. "I don't want to hurt you."

Logically, Crane knew he'd been shot, but whatever they were pumping into him through the IV in his arm made him feel pretty damn good. "You won't. Sit."

He didn't release her hand, so her climb onto the bed was the opposite of graceful.

After a couple of tries, in which he wisely swallowed his chuckle, she managed it. When she settled, she glared at him as if to say, "You made that harder than it needed to be," before she started to tell the story.

"After you . . ." Her eyes flooded, making his chest constrict in sympathy, and he squeezed her hand.

She swallowed, then said, "Passed out. The team showed up. They helped get you airlifted here to Germany. We're at Landstuhl Regional Medical Center on Spangdahlem Air Base."

The relief he hadn't put her through worse than that loosened the tie around his lungs.

He figured he'd landed in pretty good hands if he was in a U.S. Air Force hospital. It was funny; despite his time with the Marines, he'd never made it to Europe. He'd always wanted to go. See the Rhine, pay his respects at the Berlin Wall memorial, eat a hamburger in Hamburg. But there'd be time to play tourist later.

"I'm guessing they took care of Jordy?" He tried not to growl the fucker's name, but he'd thought of the man as a brother. The betrayal dug a chasm in his soul.

Rogue nodded. "Duke and Romeo stayed behind to clean up while Herc delivered the traitor."

Which left Bo and their leader, Victor. Rogue must've read the question in his eyes because she said, "Victor's on damage control, and Bo is . . ." Her shoulders gave a slight shrug. "Bo."

The former Navy SEAL was as taciturn as they came. No one knew where he went when they weren't on an op. He had a habit of disappearing.

Crane had been pissed at all of them for leaving Rogue to fend for herself. But now he wondered if he'd misjudged them. "How'd they know where we were?"

"Dafi." She scowled. "I guess I shouldn't complain since what he did saved your life, but you really should keep better company, Crane." She shook her head. "The man sold Jordan out to Victor for more money."

Her indignation made him grin. He'd known Dafi was only as good as the highest bidder. "Smart man."

Her eyes fired like she wished she could

smack him, and he chuckled. It was still fun to rile up his squirrel. "What else?"

"Jordy's aim sucked, or you're ridiculously lucky. Either way, the bullet made a clean exit. I'm sure the doctor will explain all the technical stuff to you, but surgery went well. You'll make a full recovery."

He didn't miss her gulp on the last word. Had she worried about him? Sat by his bedside? Which made him wonder . . . "How long was I out?"

"Three days."

The number proved longer than he'd expected. He palmed Rogue's cheek and asked softly, "Have you slept?"

"Some." He started to drop his hand, but she gripped his wrist as if she didn't want to let go. "Crane . . ." Her eyes misted, but she blinked them clear.

"What is it, squirrel?"

She chewed her lip and dropped her gaze to their joined hands. "Do you remember what you said to me? Before we went in the warehouse?"

Abso-fucking-lutely. Did her bringing it up

mean . . .? Hope danced in his stomach, but his answer remained clipped with caution. He didn't think the pain meds could do anything against emotional pain. "Yes."

She met his gaze again; hers swam, heavy with emotion. "You already have it." She took a deep breath. "My heart, I mean. I love you, too, Miles."

Crane didn't know if this was real. Maybe he dreamt again. Or hallucinated, his brain conjuring some morphine-induced fantasy. Because it felt surreal, he asked, "You love me?"

"Yes. Don't get me wrong, I didn't want to." He caught the exasperation in her tone. "But you made me fall for you anyway. When I almost lost you—"

Her words cut off as a sob hiccupped out of her. Unable to not touch her, he pulled her close. "Baby, don't cry." He kissed her forehead and crooned, "I'm so sorry, Rogue. I'd never leave you willingly. I promise you that."

He stroked her hair while she clung to the hospital gown over his chest. When he didn't feel any dampness from tears, he let out a small sigh of relief.

Rogue had finally opened her heart to him.

She was his. Now and always.

A sense of euphoria flitted through his body, heightened by the opioids already in his system. He wanted to celebrate her love, not dwell on what might've happened. A wild idea struck him, and he tipped her chin to look into her beautiful face.

Her eyes were dry, but he wanted to see them smile. "Marry me?"

She pushed herself upright with a snort. "I don't know if it's you or the pain meds talking."

Crane grinned at her sauciness. "It's me. Look, we're already in Europe. We can use the hospital chapel, then hit the sights as a honeymoon."

Her eyes widened. "I think you're serious."

"As a gunshot wound."

This time, she did smack him on the shoulder before her face fell, looking instantly apologetic. "Shit, I'm sorry. Did that hurt?"

"No. I'm still waiting on an answer,

Rogue." He cocked an eyebrow and would've crossed his arms over his chest if not for the IV.

She chewed at her lip again, and he couldn't help but want a taste. But first, he needed her response. Maybe it was the medication, but he didn't worry she'd say no. They'd been through too much together; he knew her inside and out. Even the parts she liked to put barricades around.

A slow smile started at her mouth and traveled up her cheeks to her eyes. The deep, smoky brown became luminous, and he knew what she would say before the word left her lips. "Yes."

Despite the hole in his side, he didn't think he'd ever felt so alive. Warmth buzzed through him like a livewire, and he cupped her neck, pulling her in for a kiss that was too many days overdue.

She softened under his touch, and he reveled in how responsive she always was to him. It made his blood heat faster than a lit match. Rogue was all his and he couldn't have asked for a better partner.

Ready to lie back and pull her on top of

him, she must've sensed his move because she broke the kiss. "Not a chance, big guy. You're on limited duty until the doc says otherwise."

Her marked stare at his junk was unnecessary. He got her point. Still, a sly grin threatened to make his lips twitch. The tent in the blanket covering his lap said he felt more than ready for full duty.

He cleared his throat. "Well, I think we're both due some time off."

Rogue nodded. "Especially since we technically saved the mission."

Her comment made him smile, but it was rueful. "Let's hope Victor sees it that way."

This time, Rogue's face held the sly grin. "He does. We had a good long talk, and things are going to be different. Even if TOP headquarters disagrees, I know he has our backs."

The gleam in her eye told Crane there was more to the story, but he doubted she'd divulge it. At least, not without a lot of convincing. He had a few ideas on how he might do that, and his blood shot south thinking about it.

Rogue's voice broke into his fantasy. "Dafi expedited the process, but they were coming back."

At her statement, the lingering distaste over his team's abandonment disappeared. Knowing he could trust them again settled something in his being.

Rogue had given him that. And it was another reason he loved this woman. She could hold her own and wasn't afraid to speak up if she sensed an injustice.

He lifted her left hand to his lips and kissed the spot where a ring would go.

First order of business.

He met her gaze with a beaming smile, full of the love he couldn't contain. "I owe you a ring."

"I don't need one." Her gaze, though soft, was filled with so many promises. She loved him. It shone in her eyes with a light that suffused him in a warmth more potent than any drug. He wasn't sure he'd ever get used to it.

"Come here." He pulled her into his uninjured side, and she rested her head between his collar and jaw.

Despite all the shit they'd been through in the last few days, he'd do it all again if it meant he'd get to have *her*. Because Rogue was worth dying for, but even more, she was worth *living* for.

As he held her close, his whole body relaxed. A deluge of contentment filtered through his veins. He couldn't wait to start their life together. With Rogue at his side, it was guaranteed to be filled with laughter, frustration, and—a chuckle rumbled in his chest—the best part? Amazingly hot sex . . .

ACKNOWLEDGMENTS

This book started as a short story for an anthology, so I have to thank Stephanie Morris for letting me be a part of that. This was my first foray into military romance, and now I'm hooked!

For inspiring this story, I want to thank all the active-duty military and veteran servicemembers. Not only for that but, thank you for your service. And to my fellow female veterans, I see you. We don't have to be as tough as Rogue to make a difference.

Going Rogue wouldn't be what it is without my amazing critique partners, M.K. and Nina. You gals are the best Dream Team ever! Thank you for helping this story be all it could be.

And thank you to my Shades of Romance ladies, whose support on this crazy writing journey but also, in life in general, means more than I can ever hope to express.

I also have to thank my advanced readers and my street team members. VIPs, you all help more than you know. I couldn't do this without you.

Finally, thank *you* for buying this book! I hope you enjoyed Rogue and Crane's adventure and that you're excited to read the rest of TOP's stories!

A NOTE TO READERS

If you enjoyed this book, please consider leaving a review. Authors are so happy when readers leave reviews because it helps spread the word about our books through the recommendation process and helps new readers decide if our books will be a good fit for them. It also contributes to our rankings on sites like Amazon, making our stories more visible to new readers. Even a one-line review makes a difference!

If you are interested in future books in this series, please subscribe to my newsletter. By subscribing, you receive an EXCLUSIVE novella featuring a woman on the run and forced proximity with a troubled military hero!

You can also follow me on social media for updates, teasers, and more.

All my links can be found here: https://linktr.ee/blyedonovan.

Thank you for reading!

xoxo,

Blye Donovan

ABOUT THE AUTHOR

Blye Donovan is a military brat and a veteran who resides in the Lowcountry of South Carolina with her husband and fur-child, Max. Besides books, she's addicted to coffee,

peanut butter, and shoes. When she's not feeding these addictions, she writes books that are romantic suspense stories featuring strong heroines and  alpha protector heroes overcoming dangerous villains. Her books are often set in small towns because she loves the atmosphere associated with them, especially when they have historic architecture. She was supposed to become a historic preservationist, but . . . writing has always been her passion. You can check out her current series, follow her on social media, and more, all at this link: https://linktr.ee/blyedonovan.